FAKE BOSS

A LESBIAN / SAPPHIC ROMANCE

GRACE PARKES

1

LEANNA FOX

"Did you think you'd ever get this far?"

Leanna snapped out of her calculations in an instant. Her blank stare had been locked on the wall, on the framed clipping of the news article highlighting her once small business the day it had opened for the very first time. Most people assumed it was displayed for sentimental reasons, but every time Leanna saw it in the corner of her eye, she knew she wasn't done yet. Even as a highly successful CEO of a thriving chain of spa and wellness centers, there was always more for her to do, create, and expand.

"Sorry!" the careful voice behind her half-whispered as Leanna turned abruptly to study her new assistant with a silent, cool gaze, taking in the woman's attire, posture, and demeanor before she answered in a steady tone.

"Of course, Miss Jenkins. Don't think otherwise if you plan to make anything of yourself in this world." She smiled gracefully.

The short woman's hair was neat and tidy, pulled up in a youthful ponytail, but it could still use a trim. Before the conversation got all mushy, Leanna got right to the point. "Were you able to collect the missing sales reports from earlier this year?"

"Of course, Ma'am!" The woman eagerly stepped forward and placed a pile of perfectly stacked papers in Leanna's hands, pulling back with a slight nod. "Here are all the reports from January to November. I've also forwarded the digital copies to your inbox. And Miss Fox?" she asked, holding in a breath as she prepared to speak.

Leanna nodded, glancing over the reports as her assistant continued, "Just now, the property owner for the new suburb location mentioned he wanted to meet with you today. I moved your schedule to accommodate it. He'll be calling you in 15 minutes, is that alright?"

Leanna waved the comment aside. "Thank you, that works just fine." She gave Miss Jenkins another sweet, perfect smile while dismissing her. "In that case, I need to prepare. Email me the updated contract for that offer."

"Right away, Ma'am!" Miss Jenkins beamed while giving her a slight nod of her head. She hurried out of the room, closing the office door carefully behind her as she returned to her own desk across the way.

Leanna's warm and welcoming business smile fell into one of relaxed neutrality as she set the documents in a bin labeled *Sales Reports* that hung in a stack of many others on her office wall. It was an easy and efficient way to keep things neat and organized, something her previous assistant had thought up before she went on maternity leave.

Her new assistant, Ruby Jenkins, was a good worker. Leanna had made sure of that when she'd hired her. But she did have to admit, it was amusing to see how hard Miss Jenkins tried. As much as Leanna appreciated the sentiment of celebrating her hard-earned success, there simply wasn't time to think about that right now. She was here, and she wasn't going to stop, not when she still had so far to go.

Leanna prepared the digital meeting in a matter of minutes, pulling up the documents and lists she had prepared days ago for this exact opportunity. With how successful The Fox Retreats had been over the past several years, she doubted that anything would prevent this new property owner from falling right into her perfectly manicured hands.

The proposed location was on the edge of a beautiful and quiet suburban community, and the dazzling lakefront property was sure to attract plenty of customers both from within and outside of the community. Leanna always made sure her chosen locations were ones she would be willing to visit herself, were she a paying customer, and this one was no different.

Within the first ten minutes of the meeting, Leanna had dazzled the man into a price well within the company's budget, promising him a yearlong membership for him and that darling wife he couldn't shut up about. It was cute, but the kind of cuteness that seemed to be masking naivety. Without a partner of her own, Leanna had no worries for such silly things. Of course, she'd still have the occasional fling here and there if things worked out with the right woman, and countless men had tried and failed to woo her, but things felt so much simpler when it was just herself and her thriving business.

Stepping out of her office brought Leanna into a whole new and bustling world, one which she navigated with ease.

The backrooms of the primary location for The Fox Retreats held countless office spaces, plenty of storage, and numerous staff rushing to keep each area stocked and cleaned, and many other members of Leanna's busy crew. She was stopped several times on her way to the main entrance to answer questions, sign a form, or direct the sweet and eager interns back to their mentors.

She smiled warmly at all of them, treating each individual with the kindness of an old and dear friend and the distance of someone that held far more power, wealth, and success than they could dream of.

She appreciated her team though. Leanna had built The Fox Retreats from the ground up, but her ever-growing team was always an integral part of that journey. Even new faces like the well-meaning Miss Ruby Jenkins were key to keeping the operation running smoothly for their clients.

"Miss Fox!" the aforementioned assistant

called out from behind, rushing to catch up to Leanna and walk in stride with her. Leanna slowed her gait a touch to give her assistant a small break but kept on walking.

"Yes? Was there something else you needed to discuss? I have a client waiting to meet with me up front."

Ruby blushed, shaking her head. "Oh, my apologies! I just wanted to see how the meeting went, but knowing you, I'm sure it went perfectly!"

Leanna nodded with a curt smile. "Thank you." She kept her gaze fixed on her assistant for a moment longer, as she was more than certain she had something else to bring up.

"Other than that, I just received word that a famous singer visited one of the original beachside locations, and the press is all over it. Did you want to take a look at the main article before our marketing team takes charge of things?"

Leanna shook her head. "Thank you, dear, but no. I trust Sebastian to handle the press releases elegantly, just as he's always done."

"Of course, Ma'am!" Ruby nodded slightly. "I'll just go finish updating that new release form then. Good luck with the client!"

As the overexcited woman headed down

another hall, Leanna couldn't help but share a small chuckle with herself. Perhaps she would need to sit down with Ruby sometime and review what procedures needed her approval. But for now, the over eagerness wasn't harming anything, and Leanna much preferred a job be done *too* well then not well enough.

Leanna gave a quick adjustment to the collar of her shirt before she stepped into the main lobby. With clients out and about on every side, it was imperative to take extra precautions to look her best as the face of the company.

The maintenance and cleaning crews were hard at work putting up a large array of winter decorations, with most of the individuals dressing up the tall and extravagant Christmas tree that had caught the eyes of several clients walking in the doors.

With a deep breath, Leanna took in the sharp scent of pine needles, waving politely to a few clients she was familiar with and some who were only familiar with her.

Waiting in a plush maroon armchair was a middle-aged woman with striking blonde hair and an elegant baby blue dress covered in delicate snowflake designs. She was busy watching the steady crowds filter in and out through the front doors, but as soon as Leanna came within view, her brilliant eyes flitted toward the CEO.

"Leanna!"

"Kristine!" Leanna called back with a beaming grin, holding her arms open wide as she approached.

Kristine rose up and pulled Leanna into a warm and enveloping hug. With her heels, she was nearly as tall as Leanna, and the two pulled back to share a quick laugh.

"Why, it's been far too long, Kristine. How was your trip to Italy? The pictures look incredible."

"Oh, it was so fabulous!" She beamed through glittering white teeth. "The food there was positively scrumptious—and the Colosseum? Gorgeous! But the spa services there, why, they don't even begin to compare to The Fox Retreats!"

Kristine laughed to herself as she settled back down, Leanna's soft chuckle merging with Kristine's honied voice as she sat in the bright white chair next to her friend.

For someone like Leanna, it was easy enough to guide Kristine through the conversation without spending the whole day there listening to her. The recounting of her trip to Italy was quick but detailed, and Leanna made sure to take note of the things Kristine liked most about the different spa services there, even as she kept changing the subject to gush about The Fox Retreats instead. Despite the praise, Leanna was always looking for ways to improve, and she trusted Kristine's opinion on these types of things.

"It really has been far too long since we've talked like this, Leanna."

"It certainly has." Leanna nodded with a warm smile. "But if I recall, you mentioned on the phone that you had something to give me in person?"

Kristine sat straight up in her chair, her dazzling grin being almost too much for Leanna to take. "Oh, yes! That was it."

She rummaged around in her bag, drawing out a crisp golden envelope with black lettering looping across the front:

Leanna Fox
CEO of The Fox Retreats &
Personal Guest of Mrs. Kristine Charleston

"Oh my…" Leanna breathed out, looking at Kristine curiously as she took the envelope from her hands. Kristine was still beaming at her.

"Well, open it, dearest! I brought it all this way!"

Leanna smiled softly, flipping the envelope over to carefully slide her short nail along the opening without damaging either the paper or her french manicure. She pulled out a beautiful card with a glittering black backdrop and gold font and designs scattered around the page.

Mr. and Mrs. Charleston would be honored by your presence at the
Charleston Christmas Gala
Saturday, December 16th
The Old Charleston Manor on Maplewood Road
Please RSVP by contacting Mrs. Kristine Charleston. Guests are encouraged to bring a plus one.

"My, what is this?" she asked, taking in each detail with a quiet sense of wonder.

Kristine leaned closer and rested a hand on Leanna's shoulder, pointing to the invitation to invite Leanna to look once more. "It's an invitation to our annual Christmas gala, of course! You know how much I've loved coming here; I just had to get Stephen to pull some strings and let me bring a few more friends this time."

Leanna blinked in surprise, glancing at Kristine with the first genuine smile she'd had all day. "Thank you, Kristine. I'm flattered that you count me among your closest friends."

"Oh, of course! And plus..." Kristine leaned in a bit closer.

Leanna put up with the moment of unprofessionalism to hear her out.

"I know you're trying to get some of the bigger investors in town to side with you on the new city center project, I thought this might be a good chance for you to introduce yourself."

Kristine pulled back, hands coming together and shoulders scrunching up to match her dazzling smile. "Oh, you will come, won't you, Leanna?"

With an endeared smile, Leanna nodded while she relaxed back into her seat, taking another look at the invitation. "As far as I know, I should be available... Do you know which investors will be there?"

"Goodness, I can't remember them all right

now..." Kristine spoke as if she were simply thinking aloud, "But I think Bob Willis will be there. And Carole Lee just RSVP'd along with her husband, Shawn. Oh! And that new singer, Tristan Lord. There's loads more, but I'd have to check with Stephen."

"Oh my..." Leanna's eyes widened. "In that case, I'll certainly want to be there. I'm sure my assistant can move my schedule around as needed." Leanna paused, pondering the proposed date a second longer before looking at Kristine with a determined look in her eye. "Count on me being in attendance."

One of Kristine's classic and excited squeals escaped her mouth as she tackled Leanna in a tight embrace. A few clients startled at Kristine's sweet but sudden outburst, but Leanna handled the encounter as she always did—with a soft and endeared smile and a quick hug in return.

Leanna carefully pulled back, rising to her feet and offering a polite hand up for Kristine as well. "Thank you for delivering it in person; I do really appreciate the sentiment, especially with how busy the place is nowadays."

"Oh of course! I'm sure the holiday season

doesn't help with that, but that's the way you like it, isn't it?"

Leanna nodded, neatly putting the invite back inside the envelope and tucking it under her arm as she escorted her dear friend to the door. "It is, but I'll certainly make the time for something like this. Once I catch up on my piles of paperwork this weekend, I'll send you an official RSVP, alright?"

"Sounds lovely, Leanna. Don't go pushing yourself too hard though. You can take a weekend off once in a while."

A soft laugh escaped Leanna before she could stop it, but she shook it away with the shake of her head. "Thank you, but I quite enjoy making sure things run smoothly. I'll be quite alright."

Kristine stopped at the door, blocking a richly dressed couple from entering, so Leanna pulled her a step closer by her shoulder to let them pass. Kristine looked a touch apprehensive, but not enough to do anything more about it. "Alright, if you say so, Leanna. I'll see you at the gala then?"

Leanna nodded once more, acutely aware of how packed the place was getting and how important it was for her to maintain her elegant image. As Kristine began to head out the door, she smiled and thanked Leanna for her pleasant hospitality.

A few steps later, she turned back just enough to call out, "Oh! And don't forget to bring a cute date! I'm sure you have them lining up for you." Leaving Leanna slightly stunned at the very sudden, and probably impossible, prospect.

"Girl, why are you calling me so late?" a tired male voice asked with an elongated yawn.

Leanna sighed, sandwiching the phone between her cheek and her shoulder while she rolled up her sleeves and stepped up to the kitchen sink. "I had some work to finish up."

"You worked until nine this evening? I know this is your business and all but take a break!"

Leanna grimaced in reply as she scrubbed at a dish. "I *am* taking a break. I'm talking to you, aren't I?"

"Yeah..." The voice fell into an all too skeptical hum. "But you're doing housework while you talk to me, aren't you?"

After a pause, Leanna went back to cleaning her dishes once more. "That's beside the point, Ty. I have a question for you, one I'm sure you'd be thrilled to discuss."

Leanna heard a crash and a yelp through the phone as her very excited friend rushed through the words "Oh my gosh, is it about your love life? Did you finally ask someone out?"

"Not quite," Leanna chuckled. "But I will have to ask someone to come to the Charleston Christmas Gala with me..."

After a few seconds of stunned silence, Ty whispered breathlessly, "You're going...to the Charleston Christmas Gala?"

"Yeah, Kristine invited me. Though I'm really only going to talk to some potential investors."

"Leanna!" Ty yelled, nearly causing her to drop her phone into the soapy sink. "You can't just turn everything into a work thing! This is your chance to take a cute girl to the most luxurious event of the year, sweep her off her feet, and—"

"But Ty..."

"No buts! We're gonna brainstorm together. And if I need to take off work tomorrow to wingman for you, I will."

"No, no. You don't need to." Leanna sighed. "Can't *you* just come as my date or something?" she asked as weariness from the day, and their current topic, crept into her voice.

"Absolutely not. Even if Tristan Lord himself

were there, I'm not gonna take this chance at romance away from you."

"But he *will* be there, Ty..." Leanna mumbled, a hint of hope in her voice.

Leanna could feel Ty's wailing soul seeping through the phone, and it caused a small smirk to blossom on her face.

"No. You can't trick me like that, it's not happening. Quick, who're you gonna ask?"

"That's the problem, I don't know."

"What about Trisha? Or that one girl from the bar you tried flirting with?"

Leanna turned off the faucet and wiped her hands on a towel, grabbing a rag to clean up just a bit more before she went to bed. "I only went out with Trisha the one night; it was fun but...I don't think she'd really like an event like this. And the girl at the bar? I never got her number, if you recall. I'm not even sure of her name."

"Yeah, because you didn't want to *enter a relationship* at the start of the busy season at work."

"It's a valid concern," Leanna retaliated.

"Not when this is probably the hundredth time you've backed out of anything that could potentially start a good and thriving relationship with a cute girl!"

"You're making it sound like I hate women."

"Nah. You're doing that to yourself. You're the one with eyes on the ladies, so who else do you know?"

"Not anyone I want to take with me to a high society event."

"Then maybe someone you don't know as well? Someone sweet, polite, eager to *at the very least* play the part of your cutie little girlfriend?"

Leanna paused, staring blankly at the space in front of her as she pondered the idea. "Hmm, play the part... I hadn't considered getting a *fake* girlfriend, but that'd probably be much easier," Leanna mused.

"No, no, Leanna, come on!" Ty pleaded over the phone.

Leanna laughed, her cleaning of the countertops slowing until she stopped altogether. "There's no way I'm getting in a relationship in just a few days, Ty. And plus, if she's willing, I think I have someone in mind that would be incredibly helpful with the investors too."

"Oh? Do tell. Is she cute?"

While putting away the last few odds and ends in her kitchen, Leanna smirked. "Yeah, I'd say so."

"Gosh, you admitted that fast, she must be *gorgeous*! Tell me, who is she?"

Leanna sighed loudly, walking over to her bedroom and flicking on the lights. "It's uh...my new assistant. I don't think you've met her."

Ty gasped loudly, "Leanna! I didn't think you'd go after your sweet new assistant like that."

"Shut it, Ty," Leanna snapped with a scoff. "It's not going to be like that. I'll explain everything to her, about it being *fake*, and that it's her choice if she wants to do it."

"Alright then, looks like I've magically solved all your problems."

Leanna rolled her eyes, setting the phone down and putting it on speaker while she changed. "Thank you, Tyler, for saving the day yet again with your expertise on wooing women."

Ty scoffed through the phone. "Who needs expertise when you've got just plain old good advice? It'll be great, okay? Treat her better than any date you've had before, and maybe she'll even stick around."

"Perfect," Leanna mumbled as she prepared her outfit for the next day. "You, more than anyone, know that I don't want that right now. She's my assistant, and we're gonna keep this a professional, working relationship. I'm not going to push anything on her. I'll just ask her tomorrow and leave it up to fate, I guess."

Ty sighed dramatically, but he seemed to be siding with Leanna by now. "Alright. And if she says no?"

"Well...then I'll make do without a date."

"Hmm, okay then." Ty went quiet for a few moments longer. Then, in a smirking whisper, added, "Make sure to call me once she says yes." And promptly, hung up.

2

RUBY JENKINS

I t had only been a week since Ruby had started her job as personal assistant to the glorious and glamorous Leanna Fox, and she already felt like she was drowning. Leanna had a presence that perfectly fit Ruby's initial image of her: pristine, precise, and seemingly perfect. Luckily for Ruby, Leanna was always kind, though she could tell that her boss liked things to be done a certain way, to be organized and well maintained, and Ruby also got the idea that she might do better slipping under the radar than trying to do something over-the-top just to please Miss Fox.

She was quite certain that her efforts to be efficient and assertive would be much appreciated, even if she longed to actually talk to Leanna and get to know her. But then, in only a few short days, Ruby was called to Miss Fox's office out of the blue, and she was sure she'd somehow messed everything up.

After double and triple checking her emails and files, Ruby gathered up every document she had promised would be done by the end of the day and headed off to the looming office before her. Every document in her arms was ready ahead of time, and she already had a plan in place for how to take care of next week's list of sales reports, incident reports, and the changing prices of the dozens of supply chain companies that Leanna bought from regularly.

Ruby did her best to dust herself off and appear as presentable and put together as she could think before knocking quickly and confidently against the office door.

"Come in!" Leanna's perfect voice rang out sweetly.

Ruby sucked in a deep breath and turned the knob with anticipation.

"Good afternoon, Ruby. How are you today?" Leanna said as she rose up from her seat.

Ruby smiled sweetly, nodding to her boss

politely and leaving the door just barely cracked behind her. She never knew if it was more appropriate to leave it open or shut for meetings like this, and she didn't know what Miss Fox preferred yet either. "I'm doing just fine, Ma'am, thank you for asking. How about yourself?"

Leanna cheerfully replied, "I'm doing quite well. I was visited by a good friend yesterday, so that was quite the pleasant surprise," she added with a soft chuckle. Leanna stepped around her desk and gently shut the door, gesturing for Ruby to take a seat. "Please, make yourself comfortable."

"Oh, thank you!" Ruby nodded, quickly handing over the documents as she sat down in the cushioned visitor chair just across from Miss Fox's desk. "Those are the reports you asked for by the end of the day. Thought you'd like them now as long as I'm here."

The quiet shock on Leanna's face showed through her usually neutral-looking expression. "Wow. I only asked for these a couple hours ago." Leanna's practiced eyes scanned the documents with precision and speed. "You certainly know how to go above and beyond expectations, Miss Jenkins," Leanna said, glancing up at Ruby with a stunned smile full of a quiet admiration.

Ruby was sure her face was glowing just a bit pinker, but she managed to whisper a quick, "Thank you, Ma'am." She still had butterflies in her stomach about what this surprise meeting could entail, but she would take a profound compliment such as that any day.

Leanna looked over the documents once more before quickly slipping them in their assigned spots in the organizer bins on the wall. She settled down in her office chair as well, pulling herself closer to the desk and fixing Ruby with a calm and studying stare.

"Before anything else, I do want you to know that you've done a remarkable job here since Kendra left."

Ruby nodded with a slightly embarrassed smile, doing her best to save face at the way Leanna's eyes seemed to latch onto every detail of her face and every movement she made.

"I appreciate you stepping up when everything is so chaotic. But I had a question for you that is... not a very traditional aspect of this type of position."

Ruby's eyes narrowed in confusion.

Leanna seemed to notice, because she quickly corrected herself. "My apologies, I should not frame this as a part of your job description, as it is very much the opposite, and certainly not required. Forgive me if this comes across as... inappropriate."

With a new sense of uncertainty, Ruby leaned back in her chair and waited for Leanna to continue.

"I have a huge and vitally important favor to ask of you, Ruby." Leanna pursed her lips, looking a bit unsure herself. It was a strange look on Miss Fox, and Ruby couldn't pinpoint whether it was because of something Ruby had done, or because Miss Fox was simply nervous. "Can I call you Ruby?"

Ruby nodded, "Of course, Miss Fox."

"And you can call me Leanna," she added with an endeared smile and a resounding comeback to her confidence.

Ruby simply nodded, politely holding her hands in her lap while her mind bounced back and forth between curiosity and worry.

After a deep breath, Leanna continued. "I've been invited to attend the Charleston Christmas Gala."

Ruby's eyes went wide.

"It seems like you've heard of it. Although I'm

eager to support the Charleston's by attending this event, Mrs. Charleston is a dear friend, and she encouraged me personally to come as a way to meet some potential investors for the bigger projects we have lined up next year."

Ruby was stunned. "Of course, an opportunity like that is... Well, you just *have* to take it, Miss— um, Leanna. I'm thrilled for you."

Leanna smiled with quiet amusement. "I'm glad you see how important an event like this is to me, and to The Fox Retreats as a whole. As my assistant, you have a very detailed understanding of how important these investors are, as well as how to go about working with them in a very professional and also...charming way."

"Certainly!" Ruby blurted out, noting the way her cheeks warmed when Leanna called her charming. "I'd be more than happy to assist you with that. I know the possibility of me coming along is practically impossible, but I'm sure I could prepare a list of talking points, and compile research on the investors you want to meet with, and—"

Leanna held up a hand, her amused smile growing a bit more uncertain by the second. "Ruby, that's the thing... What I wanted to talk with you about is... Not only would I like for you to come with me to the gala, but if you'd be willing, I'd like you to come as my date. Strictly in a professional set up, but I need to take a plus one and I don't need unnecessary drama. I thought you could be the perfect candidate for this, but I appreciate it may come as a surprise." Leanna continued on, filling the silence with her words.

Ruby rushed home immediately after the workday was over, barging inside and heading straight for her roommate's door with heaving breaths.

"Alicia, Alicia!" she called out while opening the door. "I need your help."

The first thing Ruby saw when she entered the room was Alicia's haphazardly "organized" pile of clothes to one side, and a pile of sewing projects in the corner. She had started stacking cups and mugs on the edge of her desk, and her waitressing uniform had been thrown on the back of her chair. The second thing she saw was Alicia herself, perched on the edge of her bed and wrapped up in a cozy-looking Christmas blanket.

"What's up?" she said through a mouthful of

popcorn, quickly chewing and swallowing while she made space on the bed next to her.

Ruby walked over, unbothered by the mess. She liked to keep things organized, but this was Alicia's space, and she kept the living spaces pretty neat considering the state of her room.

With her heavy breathing returning back to normal, she pulled herself up next to Alicia, noting how her friend was still wearing a tank top and her new favorite pajama pants.

Alicia must have noticed her gaze, because she quickly gave Ruby a mock pout and whispered, "Don't judge. Harvey called and gave me the day off before it gets crazy with all those scary, die-hard, holiday people."

Ruby raised a brow, glancing from the Christmas blanket to the Christmas pj's to the mini Christmas tree buried under Alicia's desk, but Alicia quickly waved her silent argument away.

"Anyway, tell me what happened? Is the new job going okay?"

Ruby shrugged, holding her hands up as a sheepish smile spread across her lips. "Kind of?"

Immediately, Alicia grabbed onto Ruby's shoulder. "Okay, something *definitely* happened. Spill it."

Ruby took a long and drawn-out breath before

mumbling somewhat unintelligibly, "My...boss sorta-askedmeoutonafakedate..."

"What?" Alicia's face was full of concern, but mostly confusion.

"My boss, Miss Leanna Fox—"

"Yeah, I know her. Like, anyone who's heard of a spa has heard of her."

"Well, she asked me to come to the Charleston Christmas Gala."

"Holy shit, did she really?"

Ruby nodded, biting her lip and scrunching up her shoulders. "Yeah. And...she wants me to be her fake date."

Alicia's jaw dropped. "No. Way."

Ruby groaned, falling back against the assortment of blankets crumbled up on the bed. "She said I could have some time to think on it, but this is so so strange... What am I supposed to do?"

"You should go, of course!" Alicia squealed.

"What?" Ruby sat straight up.

"I mean, assuming you're into girls, this could be the start to the cutest love story!"

"Ugh..." Ruby rolled her head around with a groan. "That's the thing, Alicia, I *am*. I would love to go on a date with someone as gorgeous as Leanna Fox, but she's my boss, *and* it's a fake date.

Plus, it's not like I've ever dated a girl before. I don't know how I'm supposed to act, and I might mess up horribly and make work the most awkward experience ever, or just get fired altogether!"

"So? Talk to her about it. Ask Leanna what she wants you to do exactly. Make sure your 'performance' won't impact your job. I'm sure she'd understand."

"But still...this is Leanna Fox we're talking about."

"Yeah, and you're totally gonna fall in love."

"No! She's my boss," Leanna insisted, biting back a longer retort. "I can't do this."

Alicia slipped off the bed with a grunt, dusting some stray popcorn pieces off her pants. "Bummer. I thought something like this might be good for you. It's a free date, a fancy gala which she *might* just buy you a dress for," Alicia eyed Ruby with a glimmering smirk, "and a chance to show off in front of your boss and all those hoity toity rich folks. The networking opportunities for something like this are out of this world, Ruby. So like, if things do go south with Miss Foxy, I'm sure you could easily get a new assistant job elsewhere."

Ruby grunted in reply and looked down at her

lap. "Not what I wanted to hear." But her mind was already running with the idea.

The only reason she actually got this assistant job in the first place was because she pushed herself to reach for something she didn't even think was possible. Leanna Fox? Working as her assistant was unheard of in her last assistant job. But she'd tried to be assertive and innovative, pushed herself to shoot for the stars, and when an offer for an interview later turned into an offer for a job, it all felt worth it.

She felt like she was making a difference here. Even if the prospect of working for Leanna Fox was terrifying at times, Leanna was actually quite sweet, and this would be a great chance to show off how dedicated she was to the job.

"Maybe you're right..." Ruby mumbled to herself as Alicia peeked up from her meager attempts at cleaning up.

"Wait, are you gonna do it?" she asked eagerly.

Ruby hummed, mixing the words around in her brain a bit longer before saying, "I mean, it's just the one *date*, so I think so. I'll talk to Leanna tomorrow first, but I think I want to try."

Ruby knocked on the door to Leanna's office, this time feeling much more reserved and cautious. All of the confidence behind her decision was quickly melting away with each passing second.

"Come in!" Leanna's cheery voice called out again, and Ruby let herself in before her nerves could jump out of her skin.

Leanna looked up, a brightness dawning on her face as soon as she saw Ruby.

"Ruby! Lovely to see you." Leanna rose to her feet and walked up to her assistant, taking Ruby's hand in both of her own and giving it a quick shake. "And if you're here about the favor we talked about yesterday, I'm more than okay if you need more time to think on it, please don't feel pressured otherwise."

Ruby nodded, taking her hand back once Leanna let go and quickly taking the seat across from Leanna's desk. Her boss smiled warmly, stepping back to her seat and leaning forward attentively.

"What can I do for you, Ruby?"

Ruby couldn't help but bite her lip and avert her gaze as her thoughts merged into words. "Well...it actually *is* about the favor."

"Oh, of course," Leanna eagerly responded, a

slight bit of uncertainty creeping into her voice as she sat up straighter.

Ruby made sure to sit up straight, too, stealing a curious glance at Leanna as she spoke.

"Did you want to talk more about specifics? Like I told you yesterday, coming as my date is merely to keep up appearances and have you take notes, nothing more."

With a deep breath, Ruby nodded, noting the mix of quiet nerves and dawning hope in Leanna's eyes. She had always known that Leanna had the most vibrant, piercing eyes, but this was the first time Ruby realized that they were a deep blue color. That fact alone made them almost...calming. Ruby cleared her throat.

"Yes, I did want to talk more about it. And thank you, I do appreciate the reassurance," she said with a small smile. She held her hands together tightly in her lap, doing her best to keep eye contact with her boss in a way that she hoped showed more confidence than she felt. "I know you said that I would only be your date for the gala, but I want some assurance from you that helping out in this way wouldn't impact my experience at work. I don't want to be at risk for my job if I mess something up by accident, or have things be awkward here at work after pretending to be your, um...your girlfriend."

Ruby was already sinking back into her chair, feeling the butterflies in her chest swarm up more like an army of angry crows rather than a meadow of sweet, fluttering butterflies. She did not see this coming.

Leanna was quick to answer, though, eyebrows furrowed in deep concern as she leaned across the desk. "Ruby, of course not! I would never let something like this put you at risk for your job, no matter what should happen." She smiled, her eyes softening with a practiced air about it. "And while I very much understand the potential for awkward work interactions, I assure you that I plan to continue our working relationship just as we have thus far. You're a brilliant worker, and I want to do everything in my power to ensure you continue to feel comfortable and safe working here."

Ruby gave Leanna a slight nod, the hint of a smile crossing her lips as she did so. The raging battle in her heart was a bit quieter now; knowing Leanna would be professional and kind about the experience helped immeasurably.

"Thank you, Mis—" Ruby paused. "Leanna. Thank you, that helps a lot. But, um...as awkward as it might be to talk about, what exactly would I be expected to do? A-as your girlfriend."

Leanna's warm smile didn't falter as her body and countenance relaxed back into her chair. She seemed far more comfortable with the question than Ruby had anticipated, but she figured this was a much better reaction than the alternative.

"Of course! I'm sorry I wasn't as clear about it before. The prospect of bringing a fake girlfriend to the gala was sudden for me as well. I'm not expecting much, though." She spoke matter-of-factly. "You'll come with me and act the part of my girlfriend. We'll be talking to several members of high society together, but I know you're more than capable of handling them with grace, just as you have in your job thus far. Anything you're comfortable doing to sell the story would help..." Leanna gestured to nothing in particular as her eyes meandered around the room while her thoughts came, one by one, "holding hands, hanging off my arm, maybe even a chaste kiss here or there."

Leanna paused, clearly simmering on a thought before she looked back to Ruby and asked, "You haven't done theater before, have you?"

Ruby shook her head. "No, not really. The last

time I took a theater class was when I was a teenager. But I think this seems simple enough."

Ruby bit her tongue before she risked saying anything more. Holding hands, easy. Hanging off the gorgeous Leanna Fox's arm as her cute token girlfriend, child's play. But a kiss? It was one thing to kiss a lover, or to kiss someone on a dare, but to kiss your icy boss? Ruby's stomach tightened and twisted at the thought.

"Well then, was there anything else you wanted clarification on?"

Only slightly startled, Ruby brought her contemplative gaze back to Leanna. Her eyes passed over those smiling rosy lips a little slower as she pondered on the concept of having a once-in-a-lifetime chance at a kiss.

She met Leanna's gaze, and any nervousness she had seen earlier was long gone. "N-no. I don't think so." Ruby shook her head.

"Perfect." Leanna beamed, rising from her seat, and Ruby quickly followed. "In that case, I'll let you get back to work. Don't hesitate to come to me if you have any more questions, alright?"

Ruby did her best to smile sweetly as Leanna got the door for her. She was a bit terrified at the prospect of kissing her boss. It wasn't that she *couldn't* do it, but if she kissed her once, there was a big chance that she would want to do it again... That was exactly what made her go head over heels for Chloe Richens at the Edwards' party many, many years ago. She had kissed her on a dare, and immediately, she wished she could do it again. But she didn't. Ruby had kept her lips zipped and far far away from Chloe, so it hadn't really been an issue. She may not be able to stay far away from her *boss* after potentially sharing a brief, fake kiss, but she could at least keep her lips in check. She'd done it before, she could do it again.

Leanna seemed oblivious to Ruby's plight as she stepped out the door. But as Ruby paused, simply staring blankly at the wall, Leanna spoke up carefully. "Are you alright, Ruby?"

With a start, Ruby twirled around, her long ponytail nearly whipping her in the face. "I'll do it," she whispered breathlessly, holding her breath as Leanna's eyes widened before her.

"Ruby," Leanna's brow furrowed in confusion, "are you sure?"

"I'm sure." Ruby spoke a bit louder, pouring all her confidence into her words. "I know how much an opportunity like this would help the company. I

3

LEANNA FOX

The grand ballroom of the Old Charleston Manor did not fail to impress even Leanna's luxurious tastes. It was larger than any high-end event Leanna had ever been to before, and the whole room felt like it was glowing. Everywhere she looked, Leanna saw glimmering chandeliers, intricate gold trim, and elegantly dressed men and women dancing around the uniquely patterned floor with stars glistening in their eyes. With framed archways decorating the many entrances into the main hall and a gorgeous stained-glass window covering the far wall, Leanna was certain it'd be within reason to call this gala fit for a fairy tale. Were the room not decked out in red, green, and white from floor to ceiling, she'd very well assume that she and her date had entered into a much different era.

After Ruby had agreed to attend as Leanna's date, she had told her assistant to purchase a formal dress for the occasion, and assured her it would, of course, be reimbursed. This was a company expense, after all.

The only direction she had given Ruby was to make sure the dress was either green or red, and that it would compliment the dress Leanna had already picked out for herself. While waiting for the event to arrive, Leanna did wonder if she should have just picked out a dress for Ruby too, but since there was no reason to act the part of her date outside the party, she decided that she made the right decision in the end. Perhaps Ruby would be able to make a fun outing of it, taking some friends along and trying on all sorts of fancy dresses and ball gowns. It was a childish thought, but one full of warm nostalgia and endearment nonetheless. It didn't matter though. Ruby was an adult, and were Leanna in her shoes, she'd go on her own, or perhaps bring Ty with her, and it wouldn't take her long at all to find the perfect dress.

Leanna glanced to her side and smiled warmly at Ruby. She looked back up with a beaming grin, tearing her eyes away to take in the glorious room for herself.

Ruby was hanging off Leanna's arm, holding loosely to her and leaning in slightly, the picture-perfect example of the sweet girlfriend Leanna was hoping to show off today. She had picked out a cute dress too. It wasn't as elegant as Leanna was used to, but it properly modeled her charm in a way that made her both lovable and gorgeous at the same time.

Her dress was a deep but vibrant green, paired perfectly with Leanna's crimson evening gown. The embroidered halter top was cropped at the waist, showing off just a bit of skin above the belt of her shimmering skirt dotted with tiny silver snowflakes. The embroidery on her top was in the pattern of swirling snowflakes as well. Even her earrings matched. Leanna had also taken note that Ruby's hair was done up in an intricately braided bun. It was quite impressive, but she found she almost missed the cute ponytail Ruby usually wore. Regardless, she looked elegant, excited, and beautiful. Leanna pulled her a bit closer.

"What do you think?"

Ruby looked up with a slight blush in her cheeks, a sheepish smile attempting to cover it up. "It's beautiful! I've never been somewhere so glamorous before. Have you?"

Leanna chuckled as Ruby quickly tried to correct herself.

"Sorry, of course you've been somewhere like this before. You're Leanna Fox, for goodness sake."

With a slow shake of her head, Leanna kept up her picture-perfect smile. "Actually, I've never been somewhere quite like this. I'm familiar with the world of the wealthy, but this is the first time I've been invited to somewhere with such a unique, elegant, and antique charm to it. And the first time I've had someone accompany me." Leanna's smile grew a touch warmer as she leaned closer for a quick whisper. "So please, I know we're here for work, but do enjoy yourself."

Leanna wasn't sure why, but she was quite a fan of that faint rosy blush on Ruby's cheeks. She found it quite endearing, and would no doubt ensure any onlookers thought they were the perfect couple, there was no fakeness about it.

It wasn't long before fellow guests began approaching Leanna from every direction. She had made sure to arrive early, and she wanted to greet

Kristine as soon as possible, but it was proving difficult to make it all the way across the ballroom as familiar and unfamiliar faces alike began bombarding her and Ruby with questions and greetings.

"You're Leanna Fox, correct? CEO of The Fox Retreats?" a new face asked within seconds of entering the hall. She was a taller woman with good taste in jewelry.

"Yes, that's correct," Leanna responded with an elegant smile and slight bow.

"Have you opened up any locations overseas?" a gentleman that Leanna knew must be a former client asked, but she was blanking on his name.

"Two years ago, we actually began a pilot program in eight locations overseas. They've all been doing very well. Would you be interested in attending one of them?"

Fortunately for Leanna, the man was inter-ested. His name still managed to slip her by in the end, but she was fairly certain that Ruby had jotted it down at some point.

"How long has your girlfriend been helping with the business?"

Leanna whirled around to face an army of women with various lengths of wavy blonde hair.

They all seemed to bear a resemblance to her friend, Kristine, and it didn't take long for her to recognize Penny at the front and center. She had attended The Fox Retreats a few times over the past year with her aunt.

"Penny! Lovely to see you here."

"Lovely to see you as well!" Penny replied with a bouncing smile.

Gesturing to Ruby, Leanna smiled lovingly. "This is Ruby. She hasn't been helping with the business for long, but she's already done wonders for the entire company."

"Oh, I bet Leanna's been so grateful for your help." Penny shook Ruby's hand, quickly letting her return to Leanna's side. "All Aunty Kristine ever talks about is how you work yourself to death over there, Leanna. It's nice to see you've put some time aside for other things," she said with a softened wink.

Leanna chuckled, remembering her fake romance, waving her hand to the side. "Oh, it's nothing. It's what I love. I'm just grateful to be doing it alongside someone I love as well."

The rest of the women took their turns exchanging pleasantries with Leanna and Ruby, which somehow made Ruby even more captivating with the way she shyly messed with her stray hairs and tried to sneak in a few scribbled notes of names here and there.

After the two of them managed to move on from Penny and her gaggle of eager relatives, getting across the ballroom didn't get much easier.

"How's the business been?" someone that Leanna was sure was an undercover reporter asked.

"Where *did* you find your dress?" came from someone who reminded her of Ty.

"Oh, you two are so cute together!" from a former client.

Leanna was pretty certain she even saw the fabled Tristan Lord as she and Ruby rushed by. He was crowded by adoring fans, a blur of bouncing blondes pushing their way to the front of the crowd.

Luckily for her, Ruby seemed to be managing okay. She was always either holding onto her arm or holding her hand. Anytime the people around them brought up Ruby, she seemed to hold on just a bit tighter. Maybe it was some shyness, maybe it was part of the act, but either way, Leanna thought she was doing wonderfully well. It made her think that this fake romance stuff might be just what she needed. No commitments, no ties, just company when and wherever she needed it without all of the drama. Leanna was far too busy for drama.

By the time the two of them escaped from the third guest not-so-subtly asking for a discount at The Fox Retreats, Leanna was ready for a break, and she was sure Ruby was too.

"How're you holding up?" she whispered as they rushed to the wall where they could take a quick breather.

Ruby nodded, giving her a cute thumbs up as she pulled out her tiny notebook, flipping through the pages and jotting down another handful of notes.

Leanna opened her mouth to remind Ruby she didn't need to be working herself to the bone, but a gentle tap on her shoulder pulled her mind right back to the task at hand.

The way Kristine had been talking, Leanna thought the gala would be a much more intimate event. But there were clearly high-end people from all across town and all around the world. Even so, she managed to blink away the pinprick of impatience rising up in her chest, spinning on her heel to greet the new stranger with a dazzling smile.

"Good evening, Ma'am." She smiled warmly.

"Good evening to you too! Now, who's this sweet girl with you?" the new woman asked with a pleasant smile. "I didn't know you were seeing someone!"

She was an older woman, but she had a youthful air about her. Leanna was sure this was a familiar face, but she couldn't quite figure out who.

"Oh, this is my darling Ruby." Leanna looked over to her date with a soft smile, reaching down and interlocking their fingers. She smiled back shyly. Already, Leanna was regretting not checking in with her as much as she'd hoped, but hopefully she'd have a chance after this encounter.

"And what a darling you are! A pleasure to meet you." The strangely familiar woman dressed in a shimmering silver dress nodded to Ruby, shaking her hand and looking back to Leanna curiously. "How long have you two been dating? You haven't been keeping it a secret, have you?"

Leanna chuckled, shaking her head. "No. Or at least, not intentionally." She was sure she knew this woman. Perhaps she was at a recent event The Fox Retreats had hosted. "We're trying not to make a big deal of our relationship, keep this cutie out of the spotlight." Leanna made a show of squeezing Ruby's hand with her firm strong grip and swaying into her date in what she hoped was a sweet, playful gesture. "But when we had the chance to come to the Charleston Gala? Why, I couldn't possibly have either of us miss out."

"You certainly made the right choice." The woman nodded along knowingly. "Lovely to meet the two of you, but I must be finding my husband. There's a room full of goodies on the west side of the ballroom that I'm sure he's getting lost in."

Both Leanna and Ruby laughed along with the woman, but Leanna was still searching for a way to get this woman's name out of her without being irreparably rude.

The woman gave the two of them a slight bow, and as she was turning away, Ruby reached out, gently tapping her on the arm and speaking in a sweet, but firm, voice. "Excuse me, Ma'am. I'm terribly sorry, but I am a bit new here. Could you remind me of your name before you go?"

"Oh, of course! I'm Carole Lee. Forgive my manners, sometimes we older folk get a bit too excited at events like these. You two will have to come meet my husband if you can find time this evening. As long as you aren't having too much fun on your own."

Carole gave Leanna a laughing smirk, patting

Ruby on the shoulder before parting with a pleasant goodbye.

Leanna made sure to return the pleasantries, elated at the invitation to meet with Carole and her husband later that evening. It was no wonder she hadn't recognized Mrs. Lee. The pictures Leanna had examined before had the same sharp facial structure as the woman she'd just met, but her hair had previously been much more gray. Leanna watched as Mrs. Lee elegantly walked away with her now vibrant and sleek black hair, receiving a similar amount of attention that Leanna had grown used to in the past hour or so of mingling.

By the time Leanna glanced down at her assistant, Ruby was already furiously taking notes again. She noticed the sweet features she held. A cute button nose and glimmering eyes within delicate makeup.

"Ruby," Leanna prodded, her fingertips gliding over Ruby's notably bare back before resting delicately on her shoulder. The woman didn't budge. In fact, she leaned right into Leanna, continuing to scribble away in a type of shorthand that Leanna could barely decipher. From what she could tell,

Ruby was being extremely thorough with how much she was writing down.

Leanna turned herself and Ruby away from the crowd to deter anymore conversations for the time being. "Ruby..." Leanna prodded again, squeezing Ruby's shoulder and marveling at how petite she was. Maybe she just hadn't noticed how cute Ruby's figure was before, but with the dress showing off a bit of her waist, Leanna couldn't help but think that Ruby had really gone all out to both look and act the part of Leanna's perfect little girlfriend.

With a sigh, Leanna chased the warmth from her cheeks by leaning down to better meet Ruby's eye. She gently pressed a knuckle underneath her chin, causing her startled gaze to immediately shoot upward and meet with Leanna's cool and confident stare. "I know I asked you to be thorough in your notes, but please don't wear yourself out."

"Sorry," Ruby breathed out with a wild blush.

Leanna drifted her hand up to Ruby's cheek briefly, making sure her attention wouldn't wander from her gaze in favor of writing down more about Mrs. Lee's mannerisms, or planning out how they could meet with her later that evening, or whatever else Ruby had on her mind right now.

"Thank you for getting Carole's name." Leanna smiled with her eyes just as much as her lips. "That was some quick thinking. I didn't recognize her with the new hairstyle, so I really appreciate the extra help."

She let her hand fall before the exchange lingered into territory beyond what they'd agreed to. It was certainly important to keep up appearances, but she didn't want to make Ruby feel uncomfortable, especially when this was a once-in-a-lifetime chance for Ruby to enjoy such a prestigious gala.

Ruby nodded in reply, the red in her cheeks now matching Leanna's dress.

Leanna offered Ruby her arm, which she took gladly. She leaned over to whisper in her ear, "Sorry about that. Are you doing alright? With both the notetaking and the acting?"

Ruby took a long breath in and out while nodding in reply. "Y-yeah. Yeah, I'm doing fine." She pulled herself a touch closer to Leanna, which she welcomed with a brief chuckle.

"Are you sure? We can always take a quick break before talking to more people. Perhaps we can try to find the refreshments table for ourselves.

If we're lucky, we'll run into Carol's husband there too."

Ruby seemed to ponder on this for a few seconds, and Leanna counted them lucky that no one approached in that time. Eventually, she glanced back at Leanna with a shy nod. "A break would be nice. I need some time to make sure I have everything written down. Especially the contact information. I really don't want to forget anything."

Leanna gave Ruby her best, most encouraging smile and nodded back, looking out to the crowd with renewed determination to get her dear assistant a quick break before a swarm of people descended on them once again. "Well then, let's try the pathway Mrs. Lee made for us and see if we can't indulge in a couple sweets before taking on the rest of the gala."

4

RUBY JENKINS

"Leanna Fox has a girlfriend?!" Kristine squealed, surprising Ruby out of her charade for a brief moment.

The overeager woman and presumed host of the event was wearing a beautiful white dress that made her look like a princess. A series of pale red and green ribbons were tied asymmetrically around her waist, hanging down the dress in an elegant, draping pattern.

She came right up to Ruby, grabbing her hand with both of her own. Then, seemingly deciding against that greeting, pulled Ruby into a full hug instead.

"Gosh, you're totally gorgeous!" She squeezed

Ruby tight, who, in turn, did her best to hug back. "No wonder Leanna's gone head over heels for you!"

Kristine pulled away with a beaming grin, and Leanna immediately swooped in to wrap an arm around Ruby's waist. Her glimmering deep eyes pouring with confidence and possession over Ruby. The physical touch from her confident and beautiful boss sent her face crimson red. She hated how easily her emotions surfaced. She had always been teased for her easily blushed cheeks.

It was so entirely different than Ruby had expected to actually *be* the cute couple she said she'd act as. And on top of that, she was completely convinced she wouldn't be used to the feeling of Leanna's hand on her waist, or her shoulder, or against her cheek either by the time she made it to the end of the fake date—or even after months of these types of interactions. Not that *months* were even in the realm of possibility.

"Isn't she wonderful?" Leanna asked, looking down at Ruby's striking blush. She wished she could hide behind Leanna like she could when holding onto her arm, but with Leanna holding her waist, she was front and center for everyone to see.

"She is!" Kristine nodded eagerly, taking her husband's arm while he greeted another guest. "I never thought Leanna would be one to settle down, though. How did you two first meet? And how come I've never heard about you?" she asked with a grin.

Leanna stole a glance at Ruby before she tried acting all shy and embarrassed. It didn't seem to come as naturally when she tried to force it, but apparently it was good enough for Kristine. "Well...that's a funny story. Don't know if it's really fit for everyone's ears, though."

"Oh?" Kristine immediately tore herself away from her husband, sneaking up to the couple and speaking in hushed tones. "Do tell. You can't just say something like that and not tell *me*."

Ruby blushed, managing to whisper a quiet, "You're making it sound like it was something *bad*. We just met at work."

Ruby was pretty certain she'd understood that much of their cover story. To make sure things didn't get too out of hand, the two of them had decided their story would fit with the truth as much as possible. Ruby had been working for Leanna for a couple weeks, but for their story, it would be a couple months, and it was only recently she took the new assistant position. They'd discussed several of the details, of which Ruby wasn't as sure of, but she didn't think it was supposed to be some sort of scandal. Hopefully, this was just the way Leanna talked with Kristine.

"Ruby's right." Leanna said with a sheepish grin. "It really wasn't anything bad. We met at work, and of course, a workplace romance comes with the spreading of a few rumors. It only got worse once I made her my assistant, and *not* for the reasons you're thinking, Kristine. We all know I'm a control freak but this one certainly took me by surprise."

Kristine covered her mouth to hide her excited grin.

"W-what?" Ruby blurted out quietly. "That's not what people thought, right?" She knew the scenario was fake, but even then, she couldn't help but defend her fake romance. The job she had now was very much real, and she'd put a lot of hard work into it!

"I'm sorry, I'm sorry." Leanna went on with a chuckle. "I shouldn't have said anything. Ruby's always been a very hard worker. She's organized, always gets work done ahead of time, and was honestly very deserving of the role by the time she finally got it. My only worry in promoting her was that the rumors might get worse and damage her reputation... But you're hearing it from me, Kristine, that Ruby earned this position just as anyone else would."

Ruby half expected Kristine to nod along and ask for more gossip, but as soon as she looked her way, she found Kristine practically on the edge of tears.

"Incredible. Despite everyone turned against you, you two still managed to make it work. Isn't that just the most precious love story?" She leaned back, taking a deep breath and showing off the most genuine smile for the two of them. "And don't worry, I won't spill a word of it."

For a second, Leanna seemed to be just as baffled as Ruby was, but her boss was much more practiced at covering up expressions she didn't want others to see. "Why thank you. That means a lot to both of us. And I know you've got a busy night ahead of you, but might we meet your dear husband before seeing the rest of the gala?"

Kristine wasted no time in dragging her husband over to Ruby and her boss. "Oh, of course! Stephen, meet the lovely Leanna Fox and her precious partner, Ruby..." Kristine looked at Ruby questioningly.

"Ruby Jenkins." She nodded and politely took Mr. Charleston's hand when he offered it.

Although Kristine was quick about the introductions, she wasn't as quick about the small talk. Leanna was soon trapped in a conversation with her about the possibility of The Fox Retreats creating a new luxury deluxe yearly package to somehow improve upon the luxury and deluxe packages already in place for years now.

Ruby was stuck entertaining Mr. Charleston. Or perhaps, he was entertaining her. She wasn't entirely sure.

"I hope Kristine hasn't scared you off by now. We all know what a big character she is. It's quite the charm," Mr. Charleston whispered with a healthy chuckle. "She's the most charismatic person I've met, but I've seen her scare off a number of more skittish folks with how excited she gets."

"Oh, no, I'm not about to get scared off," Ruby laughed, hoping she didn't sound as awkward as she felt. She'd managed to hold her own that night among people like Carole and a whole host of other rich folks she'd never heard of before, but she'd always had Leanna backing her up. Or rather, Leanna had been the one in charge.

Even though Leanna was right next to her, Ruby knew her attention was divided, and she'd have to handle this on her own, and with the host of the gala no less!

"I'm just teasing," Mr. Charleston responded with an endeared smile.

Ruby laughed a bit in reply, trying to strike up a pleasant conversation about how grateful she was to be meeting such a wonderful figure as Mr. Charleston.

It took her a bit to realize that the Charlestons were a bit older than she'd first thought, especially with how young Kristine acted, but it was comforting, in a way, to see through the mask. So many people, herself and Leanna included, used the spa's treatments to try and stay looking young as long as possible. Now that she thought about it, Leanna was actually quite a bit older than her. Ruby was only a year or two from 30 herself, so age wasn't as big a deal now as it used to be, but it did mean that Leanna probably had about a decade more life experience than Ruby. She'd never noticed any gray hairs or clear signs of aging from Leanna; she seemed to be immune to it. Kristine, however, probably had quite a few gray hairs she was covering up by now, but Mr. Charleston didn't seem to mind them. He reminded Ruby of own dad, maybe minus the extreme amount of wealth in his hands.

Ruby shrugged and tucked a strand of loose hair behind her ear, not sure how much she should lean into the cute girlfriend role and how much she should focus on getting information from Mr. Charleston about potentially working together in the future.

"You seem a bit out of your element here."

Ruby paused, and she felt Leanna freeze as well. Maybe she *was* listening in.

"Oh, a little, yeah." She sighed, letting a portion of her facade fall away. "I'm not as used to these events as you and your wife are. Or even Leanna, for that matter. But I'm very much enjoying it. The ballroom is absolutely gorgeous!"

Mr. Charleston nodded knowingly. "It is quite splendid. It's a shame we really only use it for large events like this."

"Well, perhaps you'll just need to start hosting more events here! I'm sure plenty of people in the community would love to use this space, especially if it's just going to be building up dust in between events."

Leanna's shoulder knocked gently into hers, and Ruby took that as a sign that perhaps she'd gone too far. Mr. Charleston seemed to be in deep contemplation, but she pushed herself to interrupt anyway.

"I-I'm sorry, Mr. Charleston. Maybe that was overstepping, I—"

Mr. Charleston shook his head before Ruby could continue. "Overstepping? I'd appreciate it if people stepped up a bit more around here. You make a fair point that this space could be much better utilized. We're here raising money for charities in our community, why not allow the community to use the space instead of simply flaunting it off to those who are far too used to the glamor to really appreciate it."

Ruby was stunned. Apparently, both Leanna and Kristine were too, as their conversation had gone dead silent.

"Do you have a piece of paper by chance?" Mr. Charleston asked with a furrow of his thick brow.

"I do!" Ruby immediately flipped open her small handbag, pulling out the notebook and flipping to a clean page with trembling hands. She handed the book over, along with her note-taking pen.

All three women waited in eager anticipation while Mr. Charleston wrote down a few words and handed the notebook and pen back to Ruby.

"That is my personal phone number. I don't give it out lightly. In fact, that's the one thing that even Kristine won't go giving out like candy."

"Honey..." Kristine complained with a deep sigh.

Mr. Charleston laughed it off. "What I'm saying is, should you come across any organizations in the community, including your own, that would like to use our space, give me a call and we'll have a chat."

Ruby swallowed away the nerves wracking through her body. "O-of course, Mr. Charleston! Thank you so much. I'll keep this safe!" She grinned in disbelief, holding up the notebook before clutching it to her chest.

"I trust you will." Mr. Charleston nodded. "I hate to say our farewells so soon, but we seem to have gathered a long line of people that, for some odd reason, want to speak with me and my lovely wife."

Ruby turned to look behind her and did find

quite a large line forming. She was very grateful they got here when they did. She quickly turned back to the Charlestons while Leanna bid them farewell.

"Thank you both so much," she said warmly. "We'll be in touch." And with that, Leanna snuck an arm around Ruby's waist and pulled her away from the crowds.

As they walked, she leaned down and placed a quick kiss atop Ruby's head. "Thank you," she whispered, hopefully completely unaware of how unable Ruby was to respond in the moment. "Let's go take a break, or at least, try to. I hope we don't get stopped on the way."

All Ruby could do was swallow and nod. After a moment, she managed to let out a soft, "That sounds great, thanks," putting all of her energy into writing down everything she could remember from the encounter with the Charlestons.

"Here you are."

Ruby took the martini glass with a shy smile, taking a small sip once Leanna sat down in one of the unbelievably cushy chairs next to her. "Thank you, I do appreciate it."

"Oh, of course!" Leanna insisted. "It's the least I can do, you've been incredible this evening. You're on fire! Are you sure you don't have a past as an actress? You certainly play the part well."

Ruby shrugged, leaning back in her chair and letting herself have a moment to relax. She closed her eyes, focusing on the sweet and tangy tastes of the lemon and syrup swirling together.

"Ruby?"

Immediately, Ruby was at attention. "Yes?" She opened her eyes to Leanna leaning across the armrest, an extravagant French martini delicately resting on her fingertips. Her eyes were smiling, and her face looked so much softer than it ever had before.

"You've truly done an amazing job, Ruby. I really mean that. You've gone above and beyond, even managed to charm Mr. Charleston into giving you his number! I can't tell you how excited I am about the opportunities that will open up for us next year."

"Thank you, but I'm just doing my best, really." Ruby shrugged, hoping she wasn't blushing for the millionth time that night.

"And you're best is exactly what I needed tonight."

Ruby took another sip of her drink, setting it aside to pull out her notebook and jot down a few more thoughts. For a few moments, Leanna let her be.

On the way over, they weren't so lucky as to make it without interruption. They ran into Bob Willis. He wasn't quite as cordial as several other people they'd talked to at the gala, but he thought his wife would be interested in a spa and wellness resort, so he had exchanged contact information.

They had also found Carole Lee again, this time with her husband. The couple was very lovely to talk to, and they definitely seemed interested in some of the new projects Leanna was planning for next year. Ruby wanted to make note of that.

Just as she was double checking her notes one last time, Leanna's hand came into view and rested atop her own. "You've done great, but this is your break. Come on, I'll grab you another drink."

She hadn't even realized she'd finished her first drink, but Ruby was grateful that Leanna got up to grab them another round. Her cheeks were burning. She didn't know why those little actions affected her so much, especially when this whole scenario was based on a fake relationship... But it did make Ruby wonder if Leanna would be her type if she ever did try dating women. She couldn't help but gaze into her eyes and stare at her soft lips. Her boss's dominant confidence was a quality that made her feel like a melting popsicle.

When Leanna returned, Ruby had put her notebook away, doing her best to actually relax and take in the extravagant scene around her.

Leanna was looking radiant as ever. Her dress was a deep red, and it paired beautifully with her short dark hair and deep blue eyes. The dress itself didn't have a lot of embellishments, but it did have a unique hi-low style in the skirt. With how many elegant folds it had, Ruby was sure that if Leanna twirled around, the dress would billow out like a giant red flower.

The top of her dress had a thin, spaghetti-strap-style that crossed in the back. The straps of her dress dipped down in a deep V neck, and she wore a simple, but pricey-looking pendant over her sternum.

They were just outside the outskirts of the ballroom, in one of the many hallways surrounding the main event, and there were chairs and couches and tables littered everywhere with some of the most luxurious seating she'd ever seen. Ruby was a bit curious if they were all antiques, or replicas, but she couldn't quite figure it out, so she dropped the question from her mind as Leanna stepped up to her seat.

"Thank you, again," Ruby whispered as Leanna handed her a full glass of her favorite lemony drink.

Leanna nodded back, settling back down with a sigh. This time, her drink was the same deep red as her dress, now with a lemon on the side.

Once Leanna set her drink down, Ruby cleared her throat and looked at Leanna quizzically. "I'm sorry if this is too personal a question..." she started.

Without missing a beat, Leanna waved the sentiment aside. "Oh, please. Ask me anything."

Ruby took a slow breath before continuing, "How come you've never been invited to the Charleston Gala before? It seems like exactly the type of event you'd be invited to every year, so I'm a little confused why this would be your first time."

Leanna nodded in reply, swirling her drink around before taking another sip. "Well, histori-cally, the Charleston Gala has been a family event. Of course, in recent years, that hasn't been the case, but I think the reason it's been so prestigious and hard to get invited to for so long is because of Mr. Charleston's father. He passed away not even a year ago, so up until this event, he was the one in charge."

"Oh, I see. I apologize, I didn't realize—"

"Ruby, dear, it's perfectly fine," Leanna interrupted with an understanding smile. "It was initially a hard time for the family, but he passed peacefully in his sleep from what I heard. And having Stephen and Kristine take over was actually quite seamless."

Ruby nodded. "That's good to hear. I never would have guessed that they only started running things this year."

Leanna took a longer drink, setting down a now empty glass with a quiet sigh. "They've been running things behind the scenes for years now. It's only now that they have the freedom to do things like invite someone from way outside the family line, like myself, or even the famous Tristan Lord."

Both of them got a good laugh at that, and it wasn't long before Leanna was inviting Ruby to get refills on their drinks.

"So, how long have you known Kristine?" Ruby asked.

"Oh, well. Kristine was one of my first customers, actually."

"Really?" Ruby asked. "That was...how many years ago did you start the company?"

Leanna nodded slowly, pondering on the number. "It's been...at least five. No, no, much longer. The first expansion was about seven years ago..." Leanna started counting on her fingers, mumbling to herself as Ruby took another drink.

She couldn't remember the last time she let herself drink freely like this, but she'd worked plenty hard today, and the evening was coming to a close soon enough. It was a nice change of pace. Plus, they had a hotel close and a cab to get them there.

"Have you enjoyed building the company from the ground up?" she asked, still intimately curious with how The Fox Retreats all began.

"Of course!" Leanna said with a beaming smile. "I've always known the value of hard work since I was a kid, but building up my company is what really made it stick with me. Originally, The Fox Retreats was just The Fox Resort. We only had the one location for a long while. I was young and hopeful, but I didn't really think anything would come from my little passion project. That is, until someone got me to change my mind."

"Really, who?" Ruby pressed, leaning over the armrest attentively.

"No one you'll know, I'm afraid," Leanna sighed. "I didn't even think to get her name that day. I was working as the receptionist, if you can believe it, and this woman waltzed right in, took a good look around the place, and told me it had *potential*."

Ruby blinked. She wasn't sure if that would be a compliment or a disgrace for the great Leanna Fox.

"I thought she was trying to tell me the place looked like a dump, but I held my tongue and tried to treat her like normal. I think she had a pleasant experience, because before she left, she told me that The Fox Resort would become something big, but only if *I* trusted that it would. Not just that it could become great, but that it *would*. An inevitability. I thought it was a load of bullshit, some fancy hope or prayer that wouldn't get me anywhere, but that belief was only the first part of my journey. In fact, I think it was the only part I needed to finally do the work I needed to make this all happen. And now, here we are."

"Wow," Ruby breathed out carefully, resting her cheek against her propped up hand as she contemplated what that line of thinking could do for her own life.

She took a bit longer than she'd expected just thinking, because by the time she focused on Leanna, she'd just finished another drink. "Gosh, and you've done it all alone?"

Leanna nodded. "Yes, I have. I can't attribute all the work to me, of course, there's plenty of incredible people that I've worked with throughout the years, but at the core, at the start, it was just me."

Ruby frowned slightly, thinking carefully before she asked, "This whole time, it's been just you? You've never had a girlfriend, or even a boyfriend, to help you out? Cheer you on?"

At first, Leanna raised an eyebrow, and then, she scoffed. "No. Haven't needed one, and frankly, I haven't had time for a committed relationship. I'm truly a workaholic."

"Yeah, that makes sense." Ruby nodded solemnly, a bit surprised at how she found herself feeling dejected at something that had nothing to do with her. "Just seems kind of lonely. With how successful you are now, you have enough people like me to delegate to. Maybe you could start looking again—"

Ruby stopped herself as Leanna sighed sharply. "No. Not right now. I appreciate the sentiment, but I'd really rather not talk about it."

Immediately, Ruby looked down, feeling the pricklings of anxiety jump up once she realized she'd gotten a bit too personal. "Sorry," she whispered.

"It's fine. If you're feeling up to it now, perhaps we can make our last wander through the ballroom on our way out? See who else we manage to run into?"

Ruby looked up and gave her best smile. "Sure, that sounds great."

5

LEANNA FOX

After their break for drinks, Leanna wasn't sure it'd be wise to talk to anymore new potential investors that evening. Ruby had gone through her list with Leanna, and she was thoroughly impressed with the number of names she got down in the end. As she dragged Ruby around the ballroom, Leanna found herself quite happy to have her familiar and quiet company amidst the bustling crowds and the slight fuzziness encroaching on her mind.

As they walked, Leanna looked for familiar faces, beaming at the chance to show off her cute new girlfriend. Ruby was shy, but sweet, when faced with the extra attention, and Leanna wanted to spoil her a little before the night was done and their ruse was finished.

"Do you want anything else before we head to the hotel?"

Ruby glanced up at Leanna and shook her head with that darling shy smile of hers. "I think I'm okay but thank you."

Leanna's perfect smile softened a little, and she reached down to delicately brush Ruby's rosy cheeks with her thumb, admiring how soft her skin was. "Hmm...then perhaps we get going for the night. What we've accomplished today will be instrumental in pushing the company to greater heights next year."

Ruby gave the barest nod as Leanna pulled her hand away. She let herself enjoy a much more excited grin, letting her pristine guise fall away in pieces as they exited the grand ballroom and made their way to the manor's entrance.

"You've truly never taken an acting class?"

With a scoff, Ruby shook her head and chuckled, "Nope."

"Just naturally gifted, then?" Leanna asked with a slight smirk, guiding Ruby to the end of the hallway. In the corner of her eye, Leanna could tell that Ruby was blushing again, and it was still as cute as ever.

"Guess so..." she mumbled, tucking a strand of hair behind her ear as her gaze drifted up to Leanna. "It was a lot easier than I thought to get into the role."

Leanna raised a brow. "Oh? Do tell."

Ruby laughed to herself, eyes darting away, then back again while her lips curled up in the most adorable smile. "I mean, you're practically like a celebrity around here. It's not too hard to *pretend* to be head over heels for you." She shrugged and looked away, that sweet smile still plastered on her face.

Leanna was amazed at how sweet Ruby could act without even *trying*. With how close Ruby was on Leanna's arm, how flushed her cheeks were, and how beautiful the entrance of the old Charleston manor looked, now seemed like the perfect time to lean in for a kiss.

Ruby had even worn the perfect shade of lipstick.

It took Leanna a few seconds to tear her gaze away, but she was sure the alcohol was just catching up with her. Better to get to the hotel and get to sleep before following through on any rogue thoughts, even if she had mentioned to Ruby that their deal might include a chaste kiss. She didn't want to overstep the boundaries, or even worse, make Ruby feel uncomfortable.

Leanna pushed her way through the double doors, adjusting her arm to hold Ruby close by her waist as they stepped into the cool night air.

Making their way to the hotel was easy enough. Leanna had planned for this, arranging for a driver to take them there, and thankfully, they left right on time to catch him.

When they arrived at the hotel, Ruby paused to look up and up and up. "Gosh," she whispered, "I've definitely never set foot in a hotel as luxurious as this. If we hadn't just come from the Charleston's manor, I'd say you were trying to win me over or something."

Leanna chuckled to herself as Ruby threw that winning smile at her once again. "Maybe I am. Gotta keep you around with how splendid a worker you are."

Ruby rolled her eyes, but she was still smiling. She hopped up to the double doors eagerly, and

Leanna had to remind herself multiple times that it would not be appropriate to grab her hand right now. Although it was possible that other patrons from the gala would be staying at this same hotel, she had no reason to play up their fake relationship just for that tiny possibility. Still, it was concerning how often she had to fight with the thought. She was a sucker for sweet, submissive girls but avoidant of relationships.

With a slight bow, Leanna grabbed the door and ushered Ruby inside, staying close as she followed after her.

The lobby was practically sparkling with grand archways, a brilliant chandelier, and an exquisite center staircase just beyond the front desk. Leanna was already taking mental note of their color choices and decor placement for her meeting with the interior design team next week.

Her hand pressed gently against Ruby's back as they stepped up to the desk.

"Good evening," Leanna said with a slow nod.

The woman at the desk was dressed in a well-fitting suit, reflecting Leanna's practiced smile with ease. "Good evening. What name is your room under?"

"Leanna Fox."

Leanna's eyes drifted to her side as she felt a pressure against her arm. Ruby was leaning against her, arms loosely wrapped around her own. Despite herself, Leanna smiled, turning back to the clerk who hummed in acknowledgement.

"Ah yes, right here. Leanna Fox. We have a double room set up for you."

"Perfect! That's with the two beds, correct?"

The clerk looked like she was about to nod, her mouth open in a silent affirmation, then her eyebrows furrowed and she shook her head. "N-no, Ma'am. It's a king-sized bed. For two." Her eyes flicked between Leanna and Ruby, panic slowly emerging from behind her cool gaze.

Ruby looked up, eyes alert, and face a blossoming blush once more. She looked at Leanna for an answer, back to the clerk, and to Leanna. Leanna, in turn, just laughed.

It was a delicate and practiced laugh, tainted with a bit of a drunk giggle, but she shook her head as her ridiculous smile settled down. "It seems there was a bit of a mix-up on one of our ends, but it's really no big deal." She waved her hand in the air, addressing the woman with a light-hearted casualness that seemed to take the edge off her worries.

"We'll take the king bed. There's still plenty of space for the two of us. Is that alright with you, Ruby?" she asked, looking back to her date and dazzling her with another smile.

It took Ruby a few moments to respond, but she nodded, her quieting blush reaching her lips as it transformed into the cutest little giggle. "T-that's fine. I'm happy to take advantage of any luxury we can get."

Ruby shrugged, and Leanna took it as an agreement, though she did wonder if there might be some uncertainty behind that laugh.

The sweet clerk was very apologetic about the mix-up, but Leanna didn't want to dwell on it. She'd slept in the same bed with plenty of women in several situations: some romantic but just as many platonic. She figured Ruby was in the same boat. Sharing the bed would be just as fake as their flirting throughout the day anyway.

Leanna graciously took the keycard to a room on the seventh floor. Together, she and Ruby decided to walk up the fancy staircase in their just-as-fancy dresses. It kept a smile on Ruby's lips, despite how tired she must be, but after one staircase, they both agreed that the elevator was the way to go.

Leanna let Ruby enter the room first, and she rushed inside, greedy to take in all the elegant details Leanna was far too used to by now. It was sweet though, the way she ran up to the middle of the room, twirled around, leapt to the window, and flopped onto the plush bed with a loud sigh.

"Oh, Leanna. This is going to be the coziest sleep I've ever had." Ruby sunk into the mattress with a pleasant little hum.

With Ruby lost in her own little world of luxury, Leanna simply shook her head with a chuckle and began her bedtime routine. Usually, she felt unable to be herself around women, however she was surprised by how comfortable she was in front of Ruby. Perhaps it was the fake element of it all, taking away all the pressure of reality.

She used the bathroom to change and freshen up, switching out her elegant evening gown for a long-sleeved, satin pajama shirt that draped halfway down her thighs. In retrospect, maybe not the most professional of sleepwear while on a business trip, but she hadn't considered that she and her assistant might be sharing the same bed, after all.

Her worries drifted away as she stepped back

to the main room to find Ruby in a large red t-shirt and black short shorts that barely peaked out underneath. Her shirt had a cute little puppy on it wearing a Santa hat. Absolutely adorable, but not at all professional.

Leanna chuckled warmly. "Where'd you get that?" she asked, gesturing to the shirt as she went about putting the rest of her things away.

"Oh, this?" Ruby pulled at her shirt to get a better look at it, her head tilted downward and her eyebrows furrowed in confusion. "I think Alicia gave it to me a couple years ago."

"Alicia?"

"Oh, my roommate. Sorry."

Leanna waved her hand in the air. "It's fine. She has good taste; it's quite adorable on you."

A quick glance informed Leanna that Ruby was indeed blushing again, now with a hand rubbing at the back of her neck. "Gosh, Leanna, you're just full of compliments tonight. Are you sure you're not the actress?"

"Sorry," Leanna whispered without any inkling of apology in her voice. "Guess it's just habit now. I'm getting good at this faking-it thing," Leanna laughed in an attempt to keep things light, her guarded walls covering her tracks, but Ruby didn't seem as receptive this time. She didn't seem offended, but perhaps...distracted?

She gave Ruby a few minutes to herself as she prepared for bed. They had already each claimed a side, and Leanna thought she would spend some time catching up on the enormous number of texts and missed calls from the evening, but one glance at her phone took all the motivation out of her. It was far too late for that anyway.

Tomorrow. Or perhaps Monday. She'd get up early and catch up on Monday.

Once Ruby came back to bed, Leanna had started to wonder if she'd offended her somehow. Maybe she wasn't as okay with this sleeping situation as Leanna'd thought. Or maybe this Alicia she mentioned wasn't just a roommate but something more.

Leanna's heart skipped a beat. Had she ever asked Ruby if she was single? She'd just assumed so, and Ruby had never mentioned otherwise, but it was always possible she just felt too pressured to deny Leanna's request.

"Ruby?" Leanna turned around to face her assistant, her blushing face highlighted by the gentle glow of the lamp.

"Yeah?"

"Are you sure you're alright with this situation? I can always just make do on the couch or the floor if it'd make you more comfortable."

Ruby's face scrunched up. "Leanna, you don't need to do that. I'm fine, I promise. There is lots of space in this big old bed!"

Leanna rested on her side, propped up against her elbow. "You're sure? I apologize for not asking this earlier, but I have been wondering if you might be uncomfortable with all this if you had a significant other back home? I can get overly focused on the task at hand, and I really should have checked—"

Somehow, Ruby's blush intensified to match her name. "No, no! I would have never done something like this if that were the case, I promise. I'm single as can be. Very single," she laughed nervously.

"Oh, thank goodness," Leanna sighed, then quickly corrected herself. "Not *glad* that you're single, of course. Just that I didn't overstep boundaries in that regard."

"N-no, no. You're fine," Ruby whispered, attempting to hide her blush with her hand. Her nails had been painted green to match her dress, fitted with little snowflakes as well.

Without thinking, Leanna reached forward and pulled the hand toward her. "These are cute. Where'd you get them done?"

"Oh, just at home. Alicia did them for me."

Leanna admired the handiwork with renewed respect toward Ruby's roommate. "Sounds like she's a good friend. You sure she's not anything more?" she added while leaning in with a smirk.

"No!" Ruby said incredulously, pulling her hand away. "Of course we talk about these things, crushes and whatnot, but she's just my best friend and nothing more."

"Alright, alright, I'll stop teasing." Leanna brought her own delicately manicured hand up to cover her soft chuckle. "She seems sweet though. Good friends are important in this dark world."

Ruby slumped into her pillow slightly. "She is, yeah. We've been friends for years now. She helped me pick out my dress, and even convinced me to come in the first place."

"Oh, really?" Leanna feigned surprise. "I'll have to thank her then, should I ever get the pleasure of meeting her."

Ruby's face broke into a beaming laugh, and she practically snorted. "Gosh, I think Alicia would collapse on the spot if she got to meet you. Not only does she think you're incredible, but she was *very* invested in our fake romance."

Leanna found herself laughing as well. It was something warm and vibrant, a part of her that she hadn't explored much. She blamed it on the alcohol again. "Do tell! I'd love to know everything you two talked about. We're fake girlfriends for the night, after all." She leaned closer at that, resting her elbow against the edge of her pillow, not quite encroaching on Ruby's side.

"Well, for starters, I was *so* worked up over having to fake kiss you." Ruby snorted again. "It feels stupid now, but I thought it'd be the end of my career if I messed it up."

"Not at all," Leanna smiled, carefully taking Ruby's hand once more. "I'd never do something like that to you." She waited a second, but Ruby just blushed back at her, averting her gaze. Leanna watched her eyes a couple moments more, then pressed her lips to the top of her hand, humming in contemplation as her eyes drifted shut.

"A *chaste kiss*...I never did fulfill that part of our agreement," she mumbled against Ruby's soft and delicate skin.

Ruby sucked in a sharp breath, but her hand

stayed rooted in place, so Leanna took that as a cue for another brush of her lips.

A part of Leanna was living in flashes of moments where she might let her lips trail up Ruby's arm, where her hands might find themselves pressed against Ruby's warm skin, or her lips might find themselves wandering to...other places. By the time she opened her eyes, Ruby's princess-like hand was still draped in front of her, but she was leaning closer than before.

Leanna looked up to meet her eyes.

Ruby's eyes were shut, her lips parted ever so slightly. Her other hand was balled up in the corner of Leanna's eyesight. Leanna carefully lowered Ruby's hand to the bed.

Ruby didn't budge. Instead, she took another careful breath. Waiting, with the scent of a lemony martini lingering on her lips.

Leanna watched those ruby-red lips, bringing a hand up to cup her cheek. She watched them until the last second, when she closed her own eyes and found an inkling of sweet and sour pressed against her own lips.

Ruby gasped, but it was a slow and yearning thing. She leaned closer, tilting her head, and reaching up to grab onto the front of Leanna's shirt. Her grip was tight and nervous, but her actions held more eagerness than wariness, so Leanna kissed back.

Her fingertips trailed along Ruby's jaw, guiding her closer as Leanna pushed Ruby's mouth apart with slow and careful movements. She cupped her hand behind Ruby's neck, and she arched up ever so slightly, chasing Leanna as she chased the gorgeous girl back.

It had been ages since Leanna had really kissed someone, and she found herself wanting more and more to just let go and have this night. She found it so hard in life to just *let go*. It would mean nothing to her the next day, and it would mean nothing to Ruby as well. After all, it was just fake, right?

They could move on with work, she could catch up on all her messages from the day before, and Ruby would remain the ever-dutiful worker with the most perfectly shaped lips of the whole Fox Retreats workforce.

She delved into their kiss, pulling at Ruby's lips with growing eagerness and enjoying their sugary taste with the hint of a smile. Her teeth nibbling Ruby's bottom lip.

By now, Ruby's grip on her shirt was so tight and insistent that Leanna found herself being pulled closer and closer to Ruby until she was practically on top of the woman. Ruby's sweet, yearning lips were pushing against hers greedily, her hands sliding to Leanna's back where she could pull her down more easily.

On instinct, Leanna followed, lips moving steadily, and heartbeat growing faster. Ruby was below her now, wearing nothing but an oversized shirt and a tiny pair of shorts. She didn't like to let herself think that Ruby was pretty—not in this way —but she really was.

She dug her nails into the pillow beside Ruby's head, pushing her lips just a bit deeper as she fought with herself. Her other hand was eager to explore, tracing down Ruby's neck and sides, cupping her waist and fiddling with the bunched-up t-shirt.

In Leanna's eyes, Ruby was beyond gorgeous right now, and Leanna wanted nothing more than to have her hands all over her. Deep down, she knew she'd regret it in the morning, even if it would be so easy to press her hand against Ruby's warm skin with one quick slip under her shirt.

But this was far different than a normal one-night stand. She'd be seeing Ruby every day after this for weeks, months, maybe even years if she kept up this level of dedication.

Her lips were so soft, and her tiny hands pulling Leanna closer made her wish they could chase this feeling further.

But they couldn't.

Leanna pulled back, moving her hands on either side of Ruby's head as her eyes shot open. She took several slow and deep breaths, taking in Ruby's petite and inviting form before chastising herself once more.

"I'm sorry," were the first words Leanna could force from her mouth. She looked at Ruby's parted lips again, then back up to her eyes. "I shouldn't have done that; it was inappropriate and disrespectful."

Ruby just blinked up at her, her entire face looking flushed as a swirling of emotions jumped around in her head.

After a moment, Leanna pushed herself off of Ruby, turning away from her and scooting as far away from temptation as she could. "It won't happen again. We should get some sleep."

Leanna waited a few moments, but Ruby didn't seem to have anything to say to her. A minute later, she finally spoke.

"Should we...talk abo—"

Leanna shook her head, cutting Ruby off. "No. There's nothing to talk about. Just forget it happened, get some sleep, and we'll get back to work in the morning. I am very sorry for getting carried away, but our professional boundaries are important to me." The cold tone of her words altered the atmosphere.

Ruby was quiet and it took some time before she finally settled down on her side of the bed. Leanna had probably ruined her working relationship with her best assistant in no more than a couple minutes.

She'd let herself have a kiss, and it hadn't even been a *chaste* one. They were both still drunk, for goodness sake.

Leanna sighed, curling up in the plush blankets that now felt cold, empty, and exposing. She should have known better.

6

RUBY JENKINS

L ight filtered in through the hotel room window, making the creamy curtains glow a soft golden-yellow. Ruby blinked the sleep away, looking from the window to the nightstand to her hands balled up around the covers.

She was surprised that she'd managed to fall asleep at all after last night. She thought she'd be lying there for hours and hours, thinking about that *kiss*.

With a slow and careful breath, Ruby uncurled her fingers, bringing one up to touch her lips. She wondered if Leanna had been looking at her lips before that moment. If, perhaps, she had also considered what it'd be like if their lips met together, just one time. She wondered why she felt so hurt. It was all fake anyway, or at least that's what she kept telling herself.

But Ruby's current issue was that she didn't want *just* the one time.

Leanna was strong, independent, wildly successful, yet still caring and kind underneath her hard exterior. She was beautiful, and her lips and hands had made Ruby feel so loved in an incredibly short amount of time. And even then, she couldn't deny the rush she felt as she pulled Leanna on top of her and when she then took charge with a vigor that made Ruby want so much more. The backlash was already far worse than the time she'd kissed Chloe Richens as a dare. This time, Leanna was in bed right next to her. All she'd have to do for another kiss was turn around and pull her close.

Her cheeks burned just thinking about it.

Her core pulsated with the thought.

After a few more moments of consideration, Ruby turned around. Leanna's half of the bed was neatly made and completely empty. Ruby sat up, looking around the room as her drowsiness left in a burst of anxiety deep within her chest.

"Leanna?" she called, her eyes frantically checking each corner of the room with furrowed brows. With no answer, Ruby threw the covers off and hopped out of bed, checking the rest of the room, and bathroom, to find it all completely empty. Leanna was gone.

Ruby grabbed at her stomach. She wanted to feel sick, but she just felt...uncomfortable. She stepped over to the couch and collapsed into it, hunching over herself as she bit her lip.

Leanna had already left, and maybe she'd already gone home. Maybe she was mad at Ruby? Or perhaps, just disappointed.

Ruby knew that actually kissing her boss was a ludicrous idea, but Leanna had been the one to actually lean in, even if Ruby had been practically asking for it...

"Gosh, I was so dumb last night. I've fucked my job up," Ruby groaned, dragging her hands down her face, lightly slapping her own cheeks in frustration. Maybe it was her secret crush, but it was probably the alcohol that was now coming back in full force. She grimaced as a dull ache began in her head.

Ruby never would have actually considered kissing Leanna without the alcohol in her system.

She didn't normally drink that much, but the night had been so surreal that she almost believed it wouldn't matter how much she drank.

Ruby lifted her head to glance at the clock on the nightstand. It was only 8:10. Not as late as she was afraid of.

Leanna could be any number of places, but her luggage was gone, so Ruby forced herself to get up and get ready for the day despite the headache looming behind her desire to distract herself.

It didn't take long before Ruby was heading to the elevator in a nice red dress shirt and gray slacks. Her shirt was the same red as Leanna's dress from the night before, and she thought it would have been cute if they'd matched, but now, she just wanted to get home.

She foolishly hoped that maybe Leanna would forget everything about their night. But, in reality, it would be even better if she *did* remember, only if it meant that she'd changed her mind.

The moment Leanna pulled away last night, Ruby's mind knew that she was right. They really shouldn't have done this, but her heart wanted Leanna to pull her close and trace her lips with her bare legs brushing against her soft skin and taunting her with the possibility of something more. Something real.

Ruby shook her head, stepping into the elevator and silently thanking the world that she had it to herself. She touched her cheek, chiding herself for how red she already was. It was one thing if she was getting all flustered over a fake relationship, but she couldn't think about *that* with her boss. But deep, deep down, Ruby hoped that Leanna did have some feelings for her, and that their kiss meant more than just getting lost in a drunken moment.

As she thought about it further, Ruby considered the possibility that her boss went down to get breakfast because she was hungry. Or perhaps, because she was taking care of something or because she had to rush back early for an important meeting. But Ruby had checked her phone multiple times. She knew Leanna had nothing planned until the afternoon, and she had no other message or indication that Leanna hadn't just left as an attempt to avoid the awkward conversation that would follow their next interaction.

Ruby stepped from the elevator and saw the hotel breakfast bar across the way. It was far nicer than any hotel she'd been to before, and it was bustling with several people that radiated elegance. She already felt out of place among them, wishing that she had Leanna to hold on to.

But Leanna was probably gone by now, and Ruby didn't want to imagine what meeting her right now would be like anyway or worse, what work would be like from now on—if she even had a job anymore. She doubted Leanna would just fire her, but it might be a mercy at this point to transfer her somewhere else, even if she'd rather stay and suffer to maintain the job she worked so hard for and maybe also for the chance to at least see the woman she feared she was starting to love.

The hotel bar was full of every kind of breakfast food and drink you could imagine, but first and foremost, Ruby needed to get herself some coffee. She'd already given her luggage to the same valet who had brought it up to her and Leanna's room yesterday. Leanna had arranged that ahead of time: taking their extra luggage directly from their homes to the hotel room and back again. Ruby had to admit that it was nice to not have to worry about it on the way home.

Instead of styrofoam or plastic, they had ceramic mugs with elegant holiday decor, so Ruby took one eagerly, preparing herself a cup and looking around at the other hotel patrons. Some were in loungewear, but it was pretty expensive-looking loungewear. Otherwise, most people were dressed in business or casual formal attire, so she was grateful for the slacks and blouse she'd packed.

Standing not far from her were two women talking casually, dressed in classy business attire. They were standing quite close, and the taller woman tucked some hair behind the other's ear, smiling with that perfect smile that made Ruby blush, even from a distance.

Ruby blinked, taking in the image of the blonde beauty giggling as Leanna leaned closer with a grin. Not only was Leanna Fox not interested in Ruby but she was also flirting with other women! What would have happened if Leanna hadn't stopped them last night? Would she have been out here flirting just the same?

Ruby's coffee was done, but she left it alone. Leanna's confident demeanor as she made advances on someone else after what they'd had last night was making Ruby sick. She tore her gaze away from the two women and quickly pushed her way past the other patrons, walking quickly toward the entrance and praying she wouldn't catch anyone's attention. She was stupid for believing her little crush could be anything more than what it was, and even more stupid for thinking Leanna might have reciprocated it, even for a moment.

The soft tapping of Ruby's feet rushing along the marble floors was quickly joined by another. She didn't look back, just waved with a forced smile to the front desk and pushed her way through the large double doors.

"Wait, Ruby!" Leanna called out.

Ruby bit her lip to keep herself from spitting back a retort. A part of her felt fiery and angry inside, but she didn't want to be. It was her own fault for believing in a stupid little lie that she'd agreed to tell in the first place.

"Ruby!" Leanna called again, grabbing Ruby's wrist as she stepped out the door.

"What?" Ruby turned to face her, a hint of malice in her voice.

Leanna furrowed her brow. "Why are you leaving? Are you okay?"

Ruby stared back incredulously, shaking her head and laughing mirthlessly as the words tumbled out of her. "Okay? Of course I'm not okay."

"I-I'm sorry. I was sure you could find your way to the lobby just fine, bu—"

"You think I'm upset because of that?" Ruby furrowed her brows, yanking her hand back and failing to not glare at her boss. "Not only did you leave me alone up there with no explanation, but I come down and see you flirting around like what happened with us meant *nothing.*"

"Ruby..." Leanna tried stepping forward.

Ruby shook her head. "No! You led me to believe that *maybe* that kiss meant something, and I feel so stupid for thinking that. I know it was the heat of the moment, and I know it's stupid to think anything otherwise. I just...I can't be here right now." Ruby looked down, clenching and unclenching her fists as the fire in her settled to a more reasonable level.

"Ruby, I am so sorry. I really didn't think all of this acting would affect you like this. As your boss, I was wrong to kiss you last night. And beyond that, I should have taken into consideration how much younger you are."

"What?" Ruby spat, eyes shooting up with her mouth agape. "Are you saying I wasn't mature enough to handle it?"

Leanna put her hands up defensively. "Whatever the reason is, you're clearly not equipped for casual things like this."

"Casual?! It wasn't meant to be anything in the first place. Were you just kissing me because you wanted something *casual* and I was the easiest catch?"

Leanna sighed, "Ruby, it wasn't like that."

"Then what was it?"

"I was drunk, we both were. I can't blame it on anything other than that." Leanna took a step forward. "I know we shouldn't have done anything, but I thought you'd at least enjoy it while it lasted and be able to move on now that it's a new day."

Ruby averted her gaze, clenching her fists again and taking two long, deep breaths. Without looking at her, Ruby spoke. "You're right. We were drunk. But it really wasn't due to anything else?" Ruby stole a glance, but all she found was her boss looking at her as if she were a child. She turned completely away from her.

Leanna took a moment to respond, but it only made her words hurt more. "It wasn't. I understand I share some blame in making you feel that way, but the best thing we can do is just move on like it never happened."

Ruby bit her lip again. She was ready to argue

on and on about how she had felt a connection last night. Even if they were drunk, she still remembered most of it. The way Leanna's hand trailed along her jaw, the way she looked at Ruby as if she meant the world to her, the way their lips had danced together, and the way Ruby hadn't stopped hoping it would happen again.

But that dream was shattering before her eyes. She forced herself to turn and look Leanna in the eye, but she knew there was unresolved frustration streaming from behind her cool gaze that she just couldn't hide anymore.

"Fine," she whispered, turning away once more. "I'll see you tomorrow."

Part of Ruby hoped that Leanna might say something else, might take back the stinging rejection, but she was silent as Ruby hurried down the steps out to the street. She didn't bother with asking Leanna for the driver that was planning to take them home. She hailed a taxi soon enough, and she didn't look back, grateful she only shed a few tears that the quiet taxi driver was kind enough not to notice.

7

LEANNA FOX

With how tidy she kept it, Leanna's office had never felt cramped before, but today, it was cramped, crowded, and frankly, quite frustrating.

Leanna had come into work an hour early, thinking she'd keep herself distracted by being in the office. But catching up on her missed messages had gone much quicker than planned, and now, she kept noticing piles of paperwork and assorted decorations that were making the space feel like a mess.

She was sure that if Sebastian or Kendra, or even Ruby, walked in, they'd think it looked immaculate, but to Leanna's trained eye, there were too many things out of place or unfinished that would make her distracted during her workday.

Leanna wondered if perhaps Ruby could help with a quick redecorating, but the idea left a sharp knot in her stomach. Kendra, her previous assistant, had always been eager to help with things like keeping Leanna's office tidy, and a part of her wished she could have that back, just until she could stop thinking about Ruby as anything but a dutiful employee. She would have to make do on her own.

It didn't take long for Leanna to tidy up the space even further, ridding herself of anything that could be distracting, and finishing up the few spare piles of paperwork. She was starting to hear people chatting and bustling through the halls, so the workday must have finally begun.

As she headed out to a meeting with the design team, Leanna found it easy to greet people like normal. She noticed Ruby at her desk, but once she looked up, she very quickly looked back to her computer, and Leanna caught the hint of a frown on her face as she stared pointedly at a document on her screen.

The knot in her stomach came back, so she

quickly pushed past the office area to one of their conference rooms.

Leanna was surprised that Ruby had been so worked up over this thing between them, but she was even more surprised at how it was affecting herself. She hadn't slept well after their night together, and after lying awake for nearly an hour in the morning, she'd decided she needed some distraction.

In hindsight, maybe she should have at least left a note for Ruby, but in the moment, she couldn't stop thinking about how much she wanted to kiss her again. Or rather, just kiss *someone*. It'd been so long, and even though Ty had told her time and time again that she should just get with someone already, it wasn't till now that she was starting to ponder it for herself.

Not that Ruby was even an option. She was her assistant, and it was better if things remained that way, so Leanna was pleasantly surprised to find the beautiful Celeste Kingsly at the hotel bar with no one as her escort. With her mixed feelings about how to handle Ruby going forward, Celeste had seemed a much better option, and much more attuned to doing something casual. And even if a long-term relationship was starting to be more appealing, it still wasn't Leanna's priority. For now, she'd let herself have some fun here and there while she thought about the possibility of something longer, maybe even call up Celeste for the night if she could manage to get off early.

She knew she would be far too distracted if she gave herself any time to think about Ruby and her ruby-red lips, so she took a breath and refocused herself as she stepped into the meeting room, determined to be as professional and productive as ever.

Leanna's plan to avoid thinking about Ruby was already going poorly. Her inbox was littered with emails from Ruby that she really didn't want to look at right now, and the design team must have consulted Ruby about her dress from the gala, since all their proposals seemed to align with those darling little snowflake patterns and the elegant green she had worn.

So far, the two of them had had a couple brief conversations, but they were awkward and stunted, and they reminded Leanna that Ruby had been right the night she asked to talk about it. The thought of doing so was making her sick, though.

The culminating event that convinced Leanna to bring Ruby in for a talk was when she got a call from Mrs. Carole Lee.

"Mrs. Lee! How have you been?" Leanna asked eagerly.

"Just fine, darling. Shawn and I have been taking it easy since the gala, but he just reminded me that I needed to call you!"

Leanna could practically hear Carole smiling across the call. "Glad to hear you're doing well, Ma'am. What can I do for you?"

"You and your darling little girlfriend were talking about expanding The Fox Retreats, correct?"

Leanna's heart jumped in her stomach at the sudden interest, but she couldn't deny the pang in her chest when hearing her mention Ruby. "Yes, we did. We're currently finishing up a detailed expansion plan for the new year, would you be interested in taking a look at it?"

"That sounds lovely, dear! Shawn and I were so impressed with the two of you, and it didn't take much looking around online to see how successful your business has been."

Leanna smiled. "Why thank you, Mrs. Lee."

"Oh, call me Carole, dear."

"Of course, Carole."

"But as I was saying, we were quite impressed with the two of you, and we'd love to take a look at that plan and discuss future investments for The Fox Retreats. I just found out my daughter visits regularly, and she insisted we help out how we can."

"Carole, that's wonderful to hear! I'm so glad your daughter appreciates our services, and I'd be more than happy to meet with the two of you whenever is most convenient."

Leanna could hear a muffled Carole speaking with someone else in the room before her voice came back loud and clear. "How about discussing this over dinner? Our treat. Would the two of you be available this coming Thursday?"

"O-oh," Leanna faltered, rushing to open her calendar. "The 21st? That should work just fine. Were you wanting Ruby to come as well?" she asked, hoping that perhaps she'd heard wrong.

"Of course! You two are so cute together, I couldn't imagine meeting with just one of you when the two of you are in this together. I insist, it'll be a lovely evening. I'll send you the restaurant details later this evening."

"Sounds perfect, Carole." Leanna forced a smile into her voice.

"Talk to you later, honey."

"Talk to you later, thanks again!"

Leanna hung up before she could mess this up any further. She slumped in her chair and pressed a hand to her forehead with a grimace. "Shit, what have I gotten myself into?" And Ruby too, for that matter.

She sighed, taking a moment to process the situation and stare blankly at the door. This was one of their biggest potential investors, and the opportunity to work with the Lees would certainly allow, and even increase, their current expansion plans, but it was all going to hinge on her and Ruby now.

Before she could overthink it, she sent Ruby a quick text asking to meet in her office, and then, she waited.

Once Ruby arrived, Leanna was already acutely aware of her stomach knotting in on itself. Their standard pleasantries were quick and lackluster, and Ruby's face was void of expression as she sat across from her.

"Was there something you needed from me?" she asked politely.

Leanna sighed, building up the courage to talk through their messy situation. "In a way... But first off, I wanted to apologize again. I promised you before that whatever occurred at the gala wouldn't affect your job, and it appears I haven't been able to make true on that promise."

Ruby's brow narrowed slightly. "How so? You said we should just move on, so that's what I've been doing. It's not as if anyone has been treating me differently, other than you, of course."

Leanna grimaced, but she knew she deserved it. "You're right." She sighed again. "I really do just want to make this better for the both of us. I wasn't lying when I said you were an incredible worker. You still are, despite everything that happened. I can tell you that I don't feel the same way as you, but I am genuinely sorry for playing with your feelings like I did."

With a huff, Ruby glanced away.

"If we work together, I'm sure we can get back to a sense of normalcy around here. I'll do all I can to make that happen."

Ruby took several more seconds to look pointedly away from her, but after not too long, she looked back, her anger softening. "I'm still not happy about what happened, but I do want to get back to normal too. To start with, can you respond to my emails? You're normally very prompt with that."

"I know, and I will." Leanna nodded, feeling more determined than she had all morning. "I'm sorry, it won't happen again."

Ruby gave a half-hearted smile, then glanced around the room. "What happened in here? It's so empty."

Leanna was surprised to have Ruby mention that of all things, but she followed her eyes and looked around as well. "I did some cleaning this morning. It felt a bit too cluttered in here."

For a few moments, Ruby just took everything in; confusion, and a touch of amusement, blossoming on her face. "A storm must have gone through since I was last here. From what I remember, it was pretty spotless before."

"You're right, it was." Leanna took a deep breath. "I've just been more distracted today."

"How come?" Ruby asked, almost back to her normal self once more. Leanna worried that her attitude would soon revert back.

"Well, for starters, I got a call from Mrs. Lee just a few minutes ago."

"Really?" Ruby's eyes went wide. "What did she say?"

Leanna hesitated, then carefully stated, "She's interested in investing. She and her husband want to meet for dinner to discuss specifics...with both of us."

Immediately, Ruby's curious eyes went dark again. "Both of us?"

"Listen, I know I said it would only be the one fake date, but the Lees were pretty convinced that we're dating, and Carole insisted on having you there."

"Just tell them I'm home sick or something," Ruby scoffed.

"I know, but you know just as well as I do that this is a once-in-a-lifetime opportunity! We've both done so much with the Lees already by introducing ourselves at the gala. If we stop now, we may never get a chance like this again."

"Leanna." Ruby narrowed her eyes. "I only agreed to the one date. I'm not doing this again. I can't afford to lose my job here, I love it."

"I know you did, but I already told them you'd be there, and this will propel the business, most certainly keeping you in a very good job."

"What?!"

Leanna grimaced. This was already going more poorly than she'd hoped. "But I promise, it's only going to be for dinner, and it should be right here in town! Nothing else, no drinking, just dinner with the Lees and taking care of business with them. If they want to do anything else, I'll just tell them we broke up. But right now, working with them is pivotal to our goals for The Fox Retreats."

"Our goals? Leanna, these are *your* goals. And I don't want to just be used as your token fake girl-friend for the sole purpose of building up your business," Ruby hesitated then added, "It *hurts*."

Leanna stopped herself from responding. She knew that this arrangement had hurt Ruby, but she hadn't fully considered what that might mean. She could see the pain in Ruby's eyes, and it pained Leanna as well.

"I really am sorry, Ruby." Leanna spoke much softer. "I would really, really appreciate it if you could be there, as my assistant, and nothing more. No kisses, not even holding hands, just come with me and be your polite and sweet self, and I think it'll work out just fine."

Ruby paused at that, but she wasn't looking at Leanna. She seemed to be deep in thought, so

Leanna let her be, watching the rhythmic ticking of the clock on her wall. Perhaps she'd need to get rid of that as well.

"After this," Ruby began cautiously, "we'll go back to normal?"

Leanna nodded. "Yes, you have my word, Ruby. Dinner with the Lees, then we'll put this all behind us."

Ruby took another long pause, one that Leanna was struggling to wait through but did anyway. After minutes of silence, Ruby looked up and nodded. "Fine, I'll do it."

8

RUBY JENKINS

R uby startled from her thoughts at a knock on the door. She was lying on her bed, staring at the ceiling and already in her pajamas, but she was grateful for the timing, as she could really use a distraction about now.

"Come in!" she called.

Alicia eagerly opened the door, dressed head to toe in her waitressing uniform and smelling faintly of freshly baked bread. "How's it going? I just got back."

"Damn, that's late for you. I'm fine, though."

Alicia paused, then looked Ruby up and down.

"You're clearly not. Any update on the boss situation?"

Ruby grimaced.

"Oh, shoot..." Alicia's eyes went wide. She grabbed a chair and pulled it over to the bed. "What's up, girl?"

With a sigh, Ruby began her spiel. "I've been meaning to tell you, but Leanna sort of fake asked me out again."

"After that fight you guys had?"

"Yeah..." Ruby nodded slowly, still trying to process the matter for herself.

Alicia immediately went into question after question wanting billion more details, most of which Ruby didn't have, but it was helpful to talk it out for a bit, especially with the dinner happening tomorrow.

Earlier that day, Leanna had texted her the restaurant address. Unsurprisingly, it was one of the most expensive restaurants in town, if not the world, and she'd been mentally preparing herself since to deal with high society niceties again without relying on Leanna like she did last time, even if she still wanted to.

"If you need, you can always just take the food and run," Alicia offered with a smirk.

Ruby scoffed. "I can't do that. Even if I'm still sort of mad at Leanna, the Lees are actually quite nice. I might as well take advantage of my own networking opportunity with them."

"You better. You deserve it after Leanna did you dirty like that."

"I mean, even if I'm not happy about it, Leanna had her reasons..." Ruby sighed quietly.

"Reasons for making out with you and running like it's no big deal?" Alicia scooted closer from her new spot next to Ruby on her bed. "Did she even apologize?"

"She did." Ruby said with a nod. "I just hate that I'm *still* crushing on her."

"Oh Ruby," Alicia pulled her into a loose hug. "You sure going to this thing is a good idea?"

Ruby shrugged and leaned into Alicia. "No, but I don't think I have much choice. It'll be over after this anyway, and then I can try to forget it even happened."

Alicia was quiet for a moment, then she spoke in a soothing tone that mixed sweetly with the smell of bread coming from her uniform. "You could still call in sick. They'd understand."

"Not unless I make myself sick just thinking

about it." Ruby slumped and let herself relax a bit more. "I already told Leanna I'd do it, so I will."

Alicia squeezed Ruby, pulling a small smile to her lips. "I just feel like you're gonna get hurt."

"Yeah..." Ruby sighed. "But I'm already hurt. I'll just stick it through, maybe even dress up cute while I have the chance."

Alicia pulled back and squinted at Ruby, "You're not just dressing up cute to impress Leanna, are you?"

Ruby scoffed. "No. I already tried that and it clearly didn't work. I just want to look nice since we're going to such a nice place."

It took a bit longer for Alicia to believe her, but in the end, she let the matter go.

Ruby was far too caught up on organizing her feelings for Leanna to really think too much about why she wanted to dress up. She thought Leanna was pretty, elegant, and intimidating in a hot kind of way, but she was also still upset with her. At least, that's what she told herself. It'd be silly to just let this go so easily. She could act respectable around Leanna, especially with the Lees, but she'd need some time to figure this out further, and she'd have plenty of time after this dinner was over.

Ruby did a quick twirl in the mirror for the third time that night, but she just wasn't quite sure if this was the right outfit.

She wasn't as dressed up as she'd been for the gala, but Leanna had told her to wear formal attire, so Ruby hoped this would work. Her hair was down, for once, and she'd straightened it too for that extra shine. She always forgot how long her hair was since she often wore it up, but she thought it'd be a nice change of pace, and maybe something new to distract everyone from the fact that she'd be desperately wanting to leave the situation from the moment she got there.

Although she liked the snowflake aesthetic from her last dress, Ruby figured she shouldn't overdo it, so she went for a more night-sky look instead. She wore a long evening gown with a slit that just barely reached up to her thigh. It was black at the bodice, and carefully blended into a deep blue at the hem. The fabric almost shimmered in the light, and the single strap was attached with a refined silver clasp. She paired the dress with simple, but classy, silver jewelry, but Ruby still felt like something wasn't quite right.

After trying on some heels, Ruby thought the look was better, but she was still struggling to know if it was good enough.

Alicia had wanted to help Ruby get ready—and possibly deter her from going again—but she was asked to cover a shift for a friend, so she'd done all the prep work she could with Ruby beforehand.

With a slight frown, Ruby rushed back to her makeup bag, trying out a different, darker shade of lipstick. It took a moment or two for Ruby to study the new look before deciding that Alicia would approve. And hopefully, Leanna would too.

Ruby checked the clock while grabbing her purse. The taxi she'd called would be here any minute. She took one last chance to mess with her hair a little before smoothing it out and deciding it would be good enough. She was far more dressed up than anything she'd been to, aside from the gala, and she kept chiding herself for hoping that Leanna would like her outfit.

"Shut up, shut up," Ruby told herself while lightly pounding a fist against her forehead. She ran past the window just in time to see a car pull up and nearly tripped on her way out the door.

It really shouldn't matter what Leanna thought

upon seeing her, but Ruby knew that deep down, she secretly hoped that Leanna might have a change of heart. She shook her head while locking the door and heading over to the taxi. It would be just one night, one dinner, one discussion about work, then she could try to forget what it was like to taste Leanna Fox's ever-inviting lips.

"Ruby! It's a pleasure to see you again," Carole said eagerly while pulling her into a sweet embrace.

She hadn't been fully prepared for such a warm welcome, but Ruby went with it anyway, hugging the older woman back and giving her a charming smile. "It's great to see you too! I was shocked when Leanna mentioned you wanted to meet with someone like me, I'm flattered."

Carole waved the comment away. "Oh, of course we'd want to see you too. You do just as much for The Fox Retreats as Leanna does as far as I'm concerned."

Ruby glanced at Leanna with an apologetic smile. Even if she did do a lot for the company, she knew it was nothing compared to what Leanna did.

Thankfully, Leanna didn't seem to notice. She simply smiled back and continued her conversation with Mr. Lee. Ruby was surprised at how similar their dresses looked this evening, almost as if they'd planned it, but Leanna's was all black, for starters. She had a high neckline with no sleeves, and a low back. The skirt of the dress was bunched up on the side so it hung in an asymmetrical ruffly pattern across the front, with a gossamer-like layer floating atop the deep, black silk.

Unfortunately for Ruby, Leanna's dress and her entire confident demeanor was only making it harder for her to focus on the task at hand.

"Shawn, you remember my lovely girlfriend, Ruby, right?"

Mr. Lee grinned with a charming air about him and offered a hand. "Of course! A pleasure to meet you again."

Ruby took the offered hand and smiled back. "Thank you, Mr. Lee."

"Please, please, we're all friends here. Call me Shawn." Mr. Lee smiled and winked in that endearing, and only mildly embarrassing, kind of way. "I would suggest we get to our meal sooner than later, though. Take a seat, and order whatever you'd like!"

Ruby turned to take a seat, but she found Leanna already pulling a chair out for her. She took it with a slight nod, hoping her blush wasn't too noticeable. She did her best to hide it behind the menu as she looked over the countless pages of options.

Leanna was seated to her left, and Ruby felt like her charming eyes were boring into her, but she didn't dare look her way. She was already struggling to focus with internal questions of what moves Leanna might make swirling around in her head, even if they were fake.

"Would you have any recommendations?" Leanna asked the Lees.

"Oh! The roast duck is quite good!" Carole offered.

"That's nothing compared to the coffee crusted elk! Plus, you'll never find it anywhere else!" Shawn added with a laugh.

Ruby looked back to the menu with even more confusion than before. She quickly scanned through the options, trying to find something familiar.

"Ruby, dear?"

With a start, Ruby looked up to see Leanna's sweet, yet confident, gaze fixed on her.

"We were just discussing appetizers. How does the sweet chili calamari sound?"

Ruby nodded. "Sounds great." But in truth, she had no idea what calamari even was. She quickly stuck her nose back into the menu to try and find out for herself.

This time, Ruby tried to tune into the conversation so she wouldn't encounter any more surprises.

"Ruby's certainly been a big help recently, I don't know what I'd do without her!"

"Oh yes, I think she's a keeper," Carole replied.

Ruby managed a quick glance and smile at Carole before looking back at the menu. The three others continued talking, but Ruby was finding it more and more difficult to focus. For now, they were just exchanging pleasantries, but soon, it'd be all business. She'd told Alicia she would try to network though, if nothing else. But the more Leanna talked about her, the more she wanted to shrink into a shell and disappear.

Once Ruby finally put her menu down, Leanna gestured for her attention, bringing a hand up to brush Ruby's hair away from the delicate array of stars crawling up her ear.

"I didn't notice till just now, but these are gorgeous, Ruby. Where did you get them?"

Ruby blushed, pulling the hair back in front of her ear. "Oh, I just found them online. I don't remember where."

Leanna hummed, still watching Ruby carefully. "Well, they're quite sweet. In fact..." Leanna leaned in close to Ruby's ear and whispered, "you look quite beautiful tonight."

Ruby's heart skipped a beat, and by the time Leanna placed a quick kiss against the side of her head, she was sure she'd be burning up with a fever before long.

The Lees were eating it up though. Both of them had practically adopted the two of them with the way they were acting, and Carole seemed to be a bit of a romantic herself.

"Oh, Leanna. You dote on her too much!" Carole chided, but she was smiling encouragingly.

"Not enough, if you ask me." Shawn grinned, catching Ruby's eye for a moment, which only made the moment far more embarrassing.

It took far too long for their food to arrive, but over time, Leanna directed less and less attention to Ruby. Maybe she was finally picking up on how uncomfortable this all was.

Ruby liked the Lees, she really did, but the thing she hated most about this situation was that she wanted it to be real. If she had an actual girl-friend who would tell her how beautiful she was and show off in front of people, she would die happy—even if it was a little embarrassing in the moment.

With those foolish thoughts, a part of her kept wondering if there was something more behind Leanna's actions than just an act, but Leanna had told Ruby multiple times that there was nothing going on.

Ruby tucked some hair behind her ear once the food arrived, taking it all in with wide eyes, and not fully knowing what each dish was.

"Are you alright, dear?" Leanna asked, leaning into Ruby's vision.

"I'm fine, yeah," she said softly, shrugging a little.

Leanna didn't seem to be convinced. She frowned slightly but passed Ruby's meal to her anyway.

Ruby ate in silence while the other three kept talking. The discussion was turning to the business side of things now, but the Lees were still acting fairly casual about it. The more they talked, the more Ruby got the idea that they wanted to build a friendship with her and Leanna as well as a business relationship.

If she were Leanna's actual partner, she'd be in no way opposed to this, but especially if the Lees were going to ask for more meetings and Leanna had to tell them that she and Ruby had broken up, maybe it'd be better if Ruby didn't get too close.

Ruby had eaten about half her meal by the time Leanna checked in again. She looked concerned, but she also looked vaguely irritated.

Ruby pursed her lips, forcing herself to look around politely. "I'll be right back," Ruby said with a forced smile. "I just need to visit the restroom."

Before anyone could stop her, she rose up from the table with a growing uneasiness in her stomach. Leanna seemed upset with her, and Ruby wasn't quite sure she wanted to be around her if that was the case. She just needed a break, before it was all just too much.

"I should go as well while I have the chance."

Ruby felt a curse nearly shoot out of her mouth, but she held her tongue and walked a bit faster.

"Don't have too much fun without us! We'll be back shortly," Leanna added, rushing to catch up to Ruby as she stepped into the restrooms that appeared far too large and grand for any establishment, let alone a fancy restaurant.

"Ruby, wait."

Ruby's heartbeat was starting to quicken, and she hoped she could just make it to a stall and lock herself in before Leanna caught up to her—even if it was a more childish thought—but Leanna's long, slender legs were far too quick for that. Leanna grabbed her wrist.

"What's going on with you?" A hint of frustration bled into Leanna's words, and it only made Ruby want to clam up more.

"Nothing. I'm just doing what I can, okay?"

"Doing what you can?" Leanna pulled Ruby back a touch, guiding Ruby's eyes to glance her way. "This is nothing like how you acted at the gala. At the very least, you can talk to me if you're bothered by something."

Ruby pulled her hand back and crossed her arms in an attempt to keep her emotions in check. "Of course I'm acting differently than I did at the gala," she mumbled, drawing her eyes away from Leanna's piercing stare. "We already talked about this, though. It's just hard, okay? Like I said, I'm doing what I can."

"You've barely said a word. Even the Lees can

see you're off, I'm sure of it," Leanna said, each word pricking at Ruby's skin.

"Well," Ruby huffed, "it seems to me that the Lees are going to want to keep up these meetings. If you're planning to keep to your word *this time* and tell them we broke up, maybe this will just be convincing evidence of that."

Leanna scoffed, stepping directly into Ruby's line of sight. Begrudgingly, she made eye contact. Leanna's eyes were just as narrowed as her own.

"I'm not talking about what happens after this," her boss said in a calm, yet seething, way, "I need you to act the part *right now*. Once the Lees agree to a deal with us in writing, I'll have no need for our frilly little fake romance they seem to love so much."

"Frilly little fake romance?" Ruby said, a blemish of exasperation in her tone.

"You and I both know that's all it is, and all it'll ever be."

"You know, the more you talk, the more I can see how much you're just using me." Ruby bit her lip as she clenched and unclenched her fists, praying their conversation wouldn't leak out into the restaurant as their volume increased.

"I'm not *using* you! You agreed to this!" Leanna spat, shaking her head in incredulous confusion.

"I didn't agree to fighting in the bathroom like we were an actual couple." Ruby frowned, struggling to keep her voice level. "Seems to me that all this *frilliness* is fake for just you, but somehow, the hurt is real, for *both of us*."

Leanna rolled her eyes, nearly shouting now. "The only way you're hurting me is by hurting the company! Couldn't you at least finish the job before running off like this?"

Ruby shook her head, taking a step back. "I'm not playing pretend anymore. I'm done, okay? You think my emotions were getting too wrapped up in this? Take a look at yourself. I just want to get back to work."

Leanna scoffed, and Ruby swore she was about to say more, but a slender red-haired woman and her daughter walked in at that moment, so Leanna shut her mouth. Her burning eyes told Ruby all she needed to know, and she felt her own stomach drop at the implication. It didn't matter who was in the right here. Ruby had messed up, Leanna was mad, and she might very well stay mad for quite some time.

Leanna's scrunched up eyes slowly reverted back to their practiced coolness, but Ruby could still see the malice behind them. Without another word, Leanna turned about and walked out the door.

Ruby watched the space where Leanna had been for a moment more, let out a deep breath, then stepped into a stall and leaned against the wall, not even aware she was crying until the hands rubbing at her eyes came away covered in tears.

She kept her crying quiet while the woman and her daughter laughed and chatted at the sinks, forcing herself to push her emotions down and down, even long after they'd left.

Ruby wondered if she needed to check on the Lees, but they were clearly Leanna's mission, not hers. If they were still there when she left, Ruby could tell them they got in a fight and leave it at that. If she was lucky, she'd never have to interact with them again, even if that thought did leave a sharp pain in her chest.

With breath after deep breath, Ruby felt herself calming down, then she was crying again, then calm once more. She had foolishly hoped that this job might resolve their differences and help her face her silly little crush, but it'd only made it worse. Leanna clearly didn't want a relationship, not that she'd ever asked for a real one in the first place, but Ruby couldn't help her stupid little inkling of hope from running her actions.

Ruby rubbed at her eyes again, staring down at the porcelain floor and the toilet that was so stupidly shiny, it sparkled. Already, she was dreading what work would be like the next day— or every day, really. She didn't want to go back, and if she was lucky, she'd wake up sick and have an excuse to wait one more day before facing what would become of her and Leanna after their disaster of a night.

9

LEANNA FOX

Starting up her own business had made Leanna struggle, cry, persist, fail, and work harder than ever, but she'd never once felt hindered by her work since the day The Fox Retreats had opened.

After meeting with the Lees and giving them an unfortunately short and abrupt farewell, Leanna had gone back to work. She worked through countless missed calls from Ty and up until the office had been dark and empty for hours, yet every time she looked over her work, she felt like she wasn't getting anything done. In fact, she wasn't getting anything outside of work done either, but every time she thought about going home, she just felt sick.

Light was gleaming through the window by the time Leanna realized she had fallen asleep at her desk. It wouldn't be the first time.

As the start of the workday approached, a bumbling of anxiety rose up in Leanna's stomach. Chattering filled the hall, and paperwork flooded her office like normal, but Ruby didn't show. Normally, Leanna would get on Ruby's case for not showing up to work without calling ahead, but the thought of calling Ruby right now was overwhelming, bringing that sick feeling front and center to the point that she very nearly threw up the meager breakfast she'd had sent down from the kitchens.

Ty called again, and this time, Leanna forced herself to answer.

"What?" she grumbled.

"Well, well, well, it's nice of you to finally pick up."

"I've been working." Leanna rolled her eyes.

"Were you working at exactly 10:28 PM when I last called?"

Leanna thought back to the night before. She had remembered when the clock turned to 7, then 8, maybe even 9 PM, but anything past that was beyond her memory. "To be honest, I really don't know. Did you have something to talk about? I should get back to work."

"I had something, but first, I wanted to ask about the *girl*. Any updates? Hopefully good ones."

"Ty, not now." Leanna pushed her hand through her hair, taking slow breaths to try and get this yucky feeling out of her. She really didn't want to think about what she'd said to Ruby.

"Mmm, if you're talking like *that*, I think now is the best time," Ty said, almost smirking right through the phone.

"But I'm actually at work right now!"

"And is she?"

"What?"

"Is she at work too? She works with you, right?" Ty asked, sounding much more casual than Leanna had felt all morning. "You should go talk this out with her if you won't talk to me about it."

Leanna bit back a retort, taking in a slow, calculated breath before straining through the words, "She's...not...here..."

Ty's pondering hum came through the phone for several seconds. "Alright then. If not her, you have me. Or perhaps you could even talk with a therapist or something. I know a couple good ones in the area."

"Therapy?!" Leanna scoffed. "I don't need therapy."

Ty sighed. "Everyone needs therapy, love."

"Yeah, right. And what would I even talk about with a therapist?"

"Maybe the fact that you might have more feelings for this girl than you're letting on?" Ty prodded.

"You're just saying that cause you want me to get a girlfriend already."

"That too, but the number of times you've talked to me about Ruby just this week has been kind of absurd."

Leanna paused at that, letting the thought of Ruby sink into her mind, but it was only making her feel sicker.

Ty, however, seemed to take Leanna's momentary silence as a success. "Well, that settles it. I'll send you some therapists' numbers, and you either call one of them or Ruby by the end of the day. Or better yet, talk to both!"

"Fine, whatever, Ty. Thanks," Leanna said with a sigh.

After a brief farewell, they both hung up, and

Leanna slumped back in her chair, scrolling aimlessly through the information Ty had sent.

Leanna had always considered therapy a respectable practice but not for her. In a way, she kind of promoted some therapeutic practices through her wellness program, but she'd never needed it, and figured she never would.

While a part of her debated what seeing a therapist would do for her image, she trusted Ty's judgment, and if he was recommending these people, they must be good. Plus, all that talk about people looking down on you for seeing a therapist was baloney anyway. If anything, it'd probably encourage other people who actually needed it to go to one, too.

Leanna still didn't completely understand why Ruby was so insistent with her feelings, even after Leanna had shut them down time and time again, but the more she let Ruby and the sick feeling linger, the more she knew this wouldn't be resolved by ignoring it. The urgency to do something gnawed at her, but the answer was growing in clarity after her talk with Ty. Even if she dreaded the idea, someone like a therapist could help her figure this whole mess out, and maybe even find out if what she felt for Ruby was contempt, lust, or maybe even love.

Leanna was slumped in her car, twiddling her thumbs in the most undignified way possible. After thinking on it for a bit longer, she'd called up Dr. Georgia Windfrey's office. She didn't expect to get an appointment for another week or so, but another client had canceled at the last minute, and Leanna had decided to take the spot that same day.

It went better than she'd expected, but now Leanna was stuck in her thoughts and struggling to do anything with them.

Talk with her.

Out of everything Georgia had said, talking with Ruby seemed to be the most important, and Leanna knew that was obvious, but it was still making her sick. Georgia had even told her those feelings would go away if she talked them out, but getting to Ruby's house was much easier than walking up to the door.

It was growing late, and Leanna was worried she'd be upsetting Ruby more by showing up out of the blue, but if she didn't go inside soon, she'd end up waiting in her car all night long until Ruby had to inevitably come out to meet her.

"If she even decides to go to work tomorrow..." Leanna mumbled to herself. But at this point, she wasn't even sure if she'd make it to work tomorrow herself.

A taller woman dressed in a waitress uniform stepped out the door, and Leanna blinked in surprise, feeling her heart sink when she realized it wasn't Ruby.

"Must be Alicia," Leanna said.

After waiting for the woman to drive off, Leanna forced her door open and trudged through the snow up to Ruby's door. It took a few more moments of consideration for her to finally knock, but Leanna had to be firm in her decision, she knew that much.

Leanna heard a muffled yell from behind the door, "Alicia, did you forget something?!"

The door swung open with Ruby reaching out with a pair of keys, but she stopped dead in her tracks when she saw Leanna.

"Hi." Leanna tried at a smile, but even she knew it was forced.

"Oh, h-hi." Ruby blinked at her, standing up

straight in that same Christmas t-shirt and shorts from their night at the hotel. Her cheeks were rosy despite being inside, and her mouth was slightly agape.

"Sorry for showing up unexpectedly, may I come inside?"

Ruby narrowed her eyes. "Is this about work? Or about...other things?"

Leanna sighed, letting her frustration about their situation fall away like the waves of the beach she loved so much. She glanced to the side, then forced herself to look back at Ruby's cool gaze. "It's about us. Please, I have some things I need to apologize for."

Surprisingly, Ruby's eyes softened at that. She didn't look particularly happy still, but she looked open.

"Okay," she whispered, holding the door open and ushering Leanna inside.

Leanna didn't realize how cold she'd been out in her car until faced with the warmth of Ruby's cute and cozy house.

"Can I get you anything? Hot chocolate, tea, water?"

"If you have some chamomile tea, that'd be lovely."

Leanna got herself situated on the living room couch while Ruby stepped into the kitchen to prepare them some warm drinks. The room was pretty simple, and there was a small Christmas tree in the corner covered in mismatched ornaments of all shapes and sizes. It made her smile.

Before long, Ruby came back with two Christmas-themed mugs and sat down next to Leanna.

"Thank you," Leanna offered with a smile, taking a sip.

Ruby was quiet for a moment longer, sipping at her own drink. It smelled like hot chocolate, and Leanna wondered if she'd ever asked Ruby about things like her favorite drink. Talking to Georgia earlier had definitely helped her realize that she wanted to, even if the prospect of making something more of their relationship was still daunting.

"What did you want to talk about?" Ruby asked softly, glancing at Leanna out of the corner of her eye.

Leanna let out a careful breath and set her cup down, doing all she could to give Ruby her full attention. "I wanted to say I'm sorry, for everything."

Ruby blinked at her, those doe-like eyes filling with a quiet curiosity and something akin to hope.

"Everything?" She set her own cup down, hands placed neatly in her lap as she listened.

"Yes, everything." Leanna's face scrunched up as she searched for the words. "You said I was using you, and I was. It was cruel of me to make light of your feelings and push you to keep doing something that was inappropriate and unacceptable in the first place."

"I mean, I did agree to it at first. That was my own choice," Ruby added softly.

Leanna shook her head. "No. I mean, sorry, you *did*, but I didn't help matters." She sighed, pushing her fingers through her hair before forcing herself to relax with another deep breath. "The thing is, I've always been like this when it comes to...liking people."

Ruby's eyebrows shot up, her face looking cuter than ever as she pondered the thought.

"Whether it's a silly little crush, or a relationship, I've never let myself want anything more than a quick fling here and there. I talked with...um, a therapist, today, and she told me I struggle with commitment. And I think I struggle to even let myself think about it in the first place."

Ruby nodded along, a bit pinker than before. "I mean, commitment is hard. I haven't been in a relationship myself in years...But I guess I didn't think about what happened with us that way."

"I wouldn't have if I were in your shoes, it's okay," Leanna offered a quick smile before returning to a more somber expression. "But I'm sorry for how I hurt you. You were also right in saying that the hurt was real for both of us at the restaurant, I just didn't want to think about it then."

Ruby paused, lowering her eyes and taking a few deep breaths. She took a moment longer, then slowly let her thoughts tumble out of her. "Thank you, but I don't think I've been completely fair with you either." She looked up, still rosy and timid. "I find myself getting crushes easily, and I thought I could handle this and not let it get out of control, but then you kissed me and...I couldn't stop thinking about it."

"Oh, really?" Leanna asked, a hint of a tease in her voice.

Ruby's lips twitched at a smile. "Come on. I've just always been like that. I don't really have a lot of close people in my life, probably because I scare them away by moving into things too quickly."

"You seem like the type of person that'd be

surrounded by others. Don't you have any family nearby?"

"Not really." Ruby shrugged. "I've got Alicia, she's basically like family. But otherwise, I moved away from home a while ago. Once and a while, I'll visit my brother if I have the funds, but it's been a while since I've seen my parents. It's complicated."

Leanna took a second to take in the new information. She hadn't expected Ruby of all people to be so isolated from others. She was absolutely wonderful, and Leanna was amazed by how the longer she spent with Ruby, the more she wanted to learn about Ruby and her life—and be someone in her life that would stay. She was stunned that other people didn't think the same way.

Leanna was surprised to be thinking it for herself, especially as it was starting to overwhelm the tight, sick feeling she'd felt in her chest all day.

"I'm sorry," Leanna whispered, reaching forward to gently place a hand on top of Ruby's. She didn't pull back. Instead, she just looked at Leanna wide-eyed once more. "That's one thing I can relate with, but for different reasons. Aside from a few, I've never really let people get close to me." Leanna paused, trying to make sense of her own feelings as Ruby stared back at her.

"It must be hard for you too," Ruby whispered.

With a sigh, Leanna nodded. "It is. I don't think I've let myself feel bad about it until now but thinking about spending Christmas on my own is starting to seem awfully lonely. You're so kind and understanding. I've been a total bitch and you're still hearing me out right now." Leanna gave Ruby a hopeful look. "If you could find it in you to give me another chance, could I spend Christmas with you?"

Ruby blinked in surprise, looking down at the ground, then at their hands. Without looking up, she slowly turned her hand over and interlocked her fingers with Leanna's experimentally, studying their hands a moment longer before looking up at Leanna again. "Spend Christmas with me? A fake Christmas or a real one?"

Leanna gave Ruby's hand a quick squeeze. "I think...I want to try for a real one."

Ruby paused, eyebrows scrunched in deep thought. Before she could open her mouth in reply, Leanna leaned a touch closer, hovering over Ruby's lap and staring directly at her growing blush.

"Ruby," Leanna began, "before you give me an answer, I do want you to know that I do like you. In a romantic sort of way." She shrugged with a soft little smile. "I know I'm awful at this sort of thing, but you've been a shining light amidst a life that was drearier and more self-absorbed than I'd realized."

It took Ruby a bit longer to take in the words and calm down her blush, but eventually, her words came out in a soft and pleading tone. "Would this be for more than just Christmas?"

"If you want it to be," Leanna replied with a warm smile, studying Ruby's face for an inkling of reciprocation, her gaze falling pointedly on her lips.

Ruby sucked in a breath, her hand gently squeezing Leanna's. Her lips were parted, on the edge of forming a coherent thought, but Leanna was beginning to form thoughts of her own. Thoughts of Ruby's sweet lips mixing with the feeling of running her fingers through that silky smooth hair of hers, and gentle reminders of those dainty little legs as Ruby shifted back and forth in front of her.

"I do," Ruby whispered, lips still parted and eyes falling shut.

The moment was feeling more and more familiar as Leanna leaned in, but this time, Ruby was leaning in as well. Their lips met and Leanna could immediately taste the sweet chocolate from her drink, twisting her mouth into a smile as she tried for another taste.

"Kiss me, *please*," Ruby pleaded quietly, garnering a soft chuckle from Leanna.

Leanna pulled at her lips once more, pushing a touch deeper and humming deeply. "I already am."

Leanna brought a hand up to Ruby's jaw, tilting her head and guiding her in the steadily growing fervor between their lips, relishing the moment before she would get lost in thoughts, hopes, and dreams of what the rest of their night could hold.

Without her even realizing it, Ruby had let go of Leanna's hand, sliding both of hers over Leanna's shoulders and onto her back where she pulled her much closer, clinging to the back of her dress shirt in the most adorable way possible.

Holding in her sliver of a smirk, Leanna slipped her tongue along the inside of Ruby's lip, causing her to shiver and lean closer as her grip grew tighter and tighter. Leanna tried again, testing the waters to find Ruby now moaning at the feeling. Her heartbeat jumped, making Leanna desperate to draw out more of those carnal and succulent sounds as she explored every part of Ruby's mouth that she could reach.

Despite Leanna's initial worries, every push and pull of their entwined lips and tongues seemed to make Ruby more confident. Leanna nearly startled from their kiss as Ruby's legs shifted and tangled themselves around Leanna's waist. Before Leanna knew it, Ruby was pulling herself right into her lap.

With her heartbeat racing, Leanna brought her hands to Ruby's slender waist, giving it a quick squeeze before slipping her hands underneath the Christmas shirt and pushing her palms up Ruby's bare sides.

Ruby gasped, arching into Leanna as her hands inched up with a burning desperation of their own, but she moaned readily as Leanna pushed her tongue against Ruby's once more.

For a quick moment, Leanna pulled back with heaving breaths to tear Ruby's shirt off the rest of the way. She took no more than a second to look Ruby up and down, acutely aware of how short her black pajama shorts were and how her chest rose and fell in quick succession, practically demanding attention even as Leanna tore her eyes away.

Leanna blinked, looking Ruby in the eye and pushing out the words, "Is this okay?"

"Don't stop," Ruby interrupted.

Leanna readily obliged, diving back into their kiss and pushing Ruby back. She eased Ruby onto the couch, her lips were burning to explore every inch and make Ruby hers tonight.

Leanna slowly slid her hand down Ruby's black shorts, slipping straight into a hot wetness that made them both quiver. Ruby's breath quickened as Leanna slowly circled around her swollen clit.

"I want you more than anything right now," Ruby moaned, softly.

Leanna continued to tease her, pushing her legs apart, kissing her deeply. Slowly removing her shorts and smothering her with sweet kisses from her lips to her burning core.

"Are you sure you want me? After everything?" Leanna teased as she nibbled skin.

Ruby's groan was enough to consent. Leanna made her way down to her thighs and back up to her wetness. Rolling her tongue over her wetness, pushing her fingers deep inside. Ruby couldn't believe what was happening, but she loved it like nothing else she had loved before.

"Oh my god, fuck me, Leanna," she growled.

Leanna thrusted deeply, fucking her slowly and hard. "You're such a good girl," she hummed, acutely aware of Ruby's desire to be dominated. It was so obvious how submissive she was in her day-to-day life. She needed to be dominated. She needed a release.

She lowered her tongue down to Ruby's swollen clit, rolling around in circles as she continued to fuck her harder. Ruby grabbed onto her hair, slowly tugging at it, enjoying every lap of Leanna's strong tongue. She started to feel a wave of pleasure run through her body, almost like electricity taking over her. She couldn't hold it in. Ruby came so hard for Leanna, tight around her fingers as they were still pushed deep inside.

"Fuckkkk," Leanna exhaled, enjoying every second.

Ruby slouched back, heavy breathing. Leanna climbed her way further up and kissed her gently.

"Would you forgive me now?" she teased, watching Ruby's post-orgasmic haze fill her mind and body with bliss.

10

RUBY JENKINS

Opening the door to find her boss waiting for a night full of wonders had already been a wild ride for Ruby but opening it once more to find a pile of goodies and gifts on Christmas Eve was somehow even more surprising.

"Holy cow, did your boss send these?" Alicia asked while leaning against the doorframe.

"I guess so," Ruby said, the corners of her mouth lifting in a pleasant smile. She picked up the giant basket, bringing it inside and away from the cold while Alicia eyed it with a growing curiosity.

"So...you gonna tell me what happened last night?"

Ruby felt her cheeks burn as she glared at her friend. "No. We just...kissed...and stuff."

"Oh my gosh. You *didn't*."

Ruby rubbed at her neck, looking to the side. "We're a thing now, okay? She opened up to me. Most people can't even open up to themselves, but she realized she needed help and saw a professional, that's admirable to me," she mumbled.

"Girl, that blush tells me all I need to know. Drop the bullshit, you got laaaaaid."

"Shut up," Ruby scoffed, her giddy smile coming back in full swing.

Leanna had sent her a basket of pastries, chocolates, an at-home spa package, some small jewelry items, and a couple of cute outfits too. She was a bit embarrassed opening all of them in front of Alicia, but she'd insisted on seeing *the haul*, as she'd called it. Plus, Ruby thought it was sweet of Leanna to do so much at the last minute.

"I think I'll make a nice lunch for us before the party. And you're welcome to it too, Alicia."

Alicia waved the comment aside. "Thanks, but I'm not about to be a third wheel on your first *actual* date with her. I'm going to my sister's anyway. You know how crazy her kids are, she'll need the help."

Ruby laughed, "You're right. Tell them hi for me."

"Of course!" Alicia beamed. "And if anything goes south, call me and I'll come grab you."

"Thank you." Ruby nodded, looking back at one of the outfits and wondering if she could wear it to the Charleston's Christmas Eve Party.

Leanna had assured her that this event would be much more informal and intimate than the last grand event. Kristine had decided to pull together a few friends for a pleasant evening together, and if Ruby was remembering right, it sounded like Kristine was pretty excited to throw something together at the last minute and haphazardly, almost giddy about it.

After putting everything else away, Ruby hung up the elegant green party dress. It reminded her of the dress she wore to the gala, but with gold accents and a few more layers to it. She was glad to have the gala as a fond memory now, even if what happened at the hotel and what happened the other night, had kept her blushing anytime she thought of Leanna.

Ruby touched her burning cheek as she

headed into the kitchen to start on a meal just for the two of them. Despite her rosy cheeks, Ruby was absolutely thrilled at how giddy, and maybe even in love, she was.

When Leanna knocked on her door, Ruby answered with a brilliant smile. Leanna was all too happy to see Ruby in the dress, noticeably checking her out before following her to the kitchen. Leanna was wearing a similar dress to Ruby's but in red. It also had gold accents, and of course she was wearing heels again. Leanna already stood several inches above Ruby, but the added height from her shoes did make things more interesting, to say the least.

Ruby was very grateful to have Leanna so impressed with her cooking. Even though her focaccia sandwiches and gnocchi soup were nothing compared to the fancy meals Leanna was probably used to, she complimented Ruby several times on them, and Ruby wondered what else she might make for Leanna in the future.

Instead of taking a taxi, Leanna drove Ruby herself, which already felt much more intimate

and caring than their fake dates. She found she
really liked it despite the butterflies it left in her
stomach.

The Charleston's house was quite grand with
high ceilings, plenty of comfy furniture, and
Christmas decor all around. It was a bit more
modern than the manor, but it still had some cozy
elements to it such as family pictures and a few
leftover toys around the corners of the main room.

The kitchen and living area were combined in
one large open space, and several guests were
already mingling. Ruby felt more at ease as she
saw a few children and teenagers in the mix. It felt
more like a cozy gathering of family and friends
than a daunting event to perform at.

Leanna offered Ruby her arm, and she took it
with a shy smile, waving to a few people that
Leanna must have known as they walked by.

"You let me know if you need anything, okay?"
Leanna whispered in her ear. "We can even leave
early if need be."

Ruby shook her head. "It's fine. It's nice here,
but I'll let you know." Ruby pulled herself closer to
Leanna, leaning against her shoulder.

"Looks like you two made up fast," a familiar
voice chuckled from behind them.

As the two of them turned around, they came face to face with the Lees. Leanna seemed more startled than Ruby, and frankly, more startled than Ruby had ever seen her.

"Oh, Mr. and Mrs. Lee, I'm so sorry how the dinner ended, I've been meaning to call—"

"It's not a bother, darling." Carole smiled.

Shawn beamed at them, a hearty laugh laced in his voice. "It was certainly shocking at the time, but we all have our issues now and again. You two must have been under a lot of stress. Grab a drink and come join us and the grandkids in one of these games!"

Ruby looked to the side to see a couple younger teenagers pulling out a brand-new board game and bickering slightly. A tired-looking woman with a baby was trying to get them to settle down. Ruby quickly looked back at the Lees and smiled. "We'd love that. Thank you for the offer, you both are far too kind."

Ruby could feel Leanna smiling at her, and though she appreciated it, she found she didn't really need it. Nearly everything here was far too expensive than anything she'd ever dream of for herself, but the people were real, if a bit different at times. Seeing all the bouncing blondes in the family, from the bickering kids to the gaggle of girls fawning over Leanna, was refreshing, and they all felt more and more familiar as the night went on.

"Want to really make an impression on the girls chasing me down?" Leanna whispered to Ruby as she eyed Penny Charleston and her crew giggling about something in the corner. Leanna whispered something more, and Ruby covered her blush with a hand, giving Leanna a shy nod.

In one swift movement, Leanna put a hand on Ruby's back and led her down into a graceful dip. She leaned in and pressed her lips softly against Ruby's, and she pressed back with a beaming smile.

The girls in the corner erupted into a chorus of excited giggles. Ruby couldn't help but join in, opening her eyes to see Leanna grinning at her.

It wasn't long after their little show that Kristine came running up to pull the two of them into a hug. "Oh, Merry Christmas, you two lovebirds! So, so glad you could make it!"

"I'm happy to be counted among your closest friends, Kristine. It's an honor," Leanna said warmly.

"Of course, sweetheart!"

"And thank you for having me again, Kristine," Ruby added, relaxing against Leanna's arm again once Kristine had let them go. "Your entire family is quite lovely."

"Oh, aren't they? It's usually fairly crazy for us during the holidays, but I thought having a few extra friends here might help them all behave."

After Kristine was dragged off to greet another guest, Leanna took Ruby to the kitchen to grab a few treats for themselves. They sat side by side, meeting with countless other friends of the Charlestons while periodically being bombarded with a child running through or an invitation to join in on a game.

Ruby was surprised by how much she was enjoying herself. Even as the night began to wane and Ruby found herself growing tired, she simply snuggled up next to Leanna who readily put an arm around her shoulder, pulling Ruby close.

When the Lees came back around, they still thought Ruby and Leanna were the most adorable couple. Ruby also found herself getting several compliments on the dress throughout the night.

It was a bit strange to go straight from being a fake couple to being a real couple, but the transition felt nearly seamless aside from their initial struggles. Leanna rubbed Ruby's shoulder as she talked with another client whose name Ruby couldn't remember, but she was relieved that she didn't need to. This wasn't a job anymore, this was a life, one that she could try and make with Leanna.

Ruby must have dozed off at one point, because she blinked her eyes open to Leanna's soft voice whispering in her ear, "Should we head home? You seem tired."

After sitting up straight, Ruby turned to her date, asking softly, "Yours or mine?"

Leanna grinned, shaking her head with a soft laugh. "It doesn't matter to me. Wherever you'll be."

The two of them got up and said their good-byes to the Charlestons and the Lees and whoever else they happened to pass by. Within another minute or two, Ruby was wide awake, especially as they stepped out into the chilly winter air.

"Somehow, I always forget it's winter until I step outside." Ruby looked around at the softly falling snow in awe, holding and rubbing her arms to keep them warm. It was quiet too, the city strangely surreal and calm as children and families all around waited for Christmas morning to come.

"Here, I'll keep you warm," Leanna offered, putting an arm around Ruby's shoulder and bringing her coat along with it.

Ruby happily leaned into Leanna, putting an arm around her back to fit herself snugly between the coat and Leanna's arms. "Thank you," she whispered. "I haven't had a Christmas Eve quite this magical in a long time."

"Oh really?" Leanna asked as they walked slowly down the street to Leanna's car. "Well, it isn't Christmas Eve anymore, darling. It's after midnight after all."

Ruby blinked up at Leanna in surprise, pulling herself closer to keep warm. "Really?"

Leanna nodded, reaching out to cup Ruby's jaw as the two of them stopped in their tracks. She rubbed her thumb against Ruby's cheek, teasing at her cute little earrings with a slight grin.

Ruby blushed, her breath coming out in small puffs. "Wow. Looks like we'll get to spend all of Christmas together, from the first stroke of midnight." She beamed. "Did you ever think we'd get this far?"

Leanna paused. "What do you mean?" she asked softly.

"Well, just that something like this could work between us after everything we've been through."

"I guess I didn't," Leanna contemplated. "But I think that's the beauty of what we have now. We both worked for something better, and even though it took some of us longer than others..." Leanna rolled her eyes as Ruby laughed along with her.

"Don't be so hard on yourself, it's in the past."

"I know. I'm just glad we have this now. And even if we don't know what the future holds, I know I want to spend it with you."

Ruby leaned closer to Leanna, pushing up on her tiptoes. "Me too," she whispered, her eyes fluttering shut as she leaned in for a kiss.

Leanna met her halfway, smiling slightly as she pulled Ruby closer by her waist, lips delicately dancing in the moonlight. Ruby hummed, letting Leanna wrap her up completely. She was warm here, and she was happy. And despite the cold, she couldn't help but feel that she was home.

EPILOGUE

Three Years Later

After signing a contract with the Lees three years ago, the success of The Fox Retreats had skyrocketed beyond what Leanna and Ruby thought was even possible. They now had locations all across the Americas, Europe, and even a few scattered throughout Asia. They'd partnered with a handful of travel agencies just a few months ago to get their deluxe island resort packages in order, and they already had hundreds of pre-orders lined up since announcing the initiative just one week ago.

Ruby's growing expertise in the wellness industry, as well as her familiarity with a world beyond the wealthy, had helped The Fox Retreats expand and offer more affordable options for the general population as well as the rich.

Leanna had continued meeting with Georgia for therapy, and it quickly gave her the idea to partner with local businesses to implement healthy work practices and company-sponsored events and retreats, leading to even more exposure for the company.

Before their Hawaii location opened up, Leanna had decided to surprise Ruby and take her there on vacation. It was Christmas Eve, so similar to their Christmas Eve night that first year. But instead of city buildings surrounding them, there were palm trees, an ocean breeze, and the gentle lapping of waves in the distance.

"You know, I always wanted to come to Hawaii as a kid," Ruby said, chuckling to herself, swirling her lemon drop martini as she watched the sun dipping gracefully into the ocean.

"Really?" Leanna asked.

Ruby hummed in agreement, taking a sip of her drink.

"I would have taken you here earlier if I had known." Leanna reached across the table and rested her hand on Ruby's, drawing her attention away from the sea.

"Oh, but visiting now makes it special!" Ruby squeezed Leanna's hand with a beaming smile. "It's our anniversary, after all."

"It is, but I still can't believe it's been three whole years." Leanna took a quick sip of her drink. "With your help, The Fox Retreats has done so much better than it ever did when I was on my own."

Ruby shrugged, a shy blush on her cheeks. "I didn't do much, really. You were the one who started it all."

"And you were the one who started this." Leanna squeezed her hand again. "Between us."

Ruby smiled, but this time, she set her drink down and leaned across the table for a quick kiss, which Leanna happily obliged.

"Come on," Leanna said, pulling the two of them up and walking over to the railing facing the beach, hand in hand.

Ruby started swinging their hands back and forth, and Leanna joined in, enjoying Ruby's darling smile.

"What about this place caught your eye?" Leanna asked.

"For the resort or when I was a kid?" Ruby slowed their hands, pulling herself close to Leanna and leaning against her arm.

Leanna shrugged. "Both, I guess."

Ruby sighed and looked back out at the ocean, her lips humming softly as she pondered. "I think it's because places like this make you feel like you're in another world. All those built-up stresses just wash away, and everything's so quiet. It's magical." Ruby glanced at Leanna with some pink in her cheeks. "Or maybe, I just feel like that because you're here with me," Ruby teased.

Leanna smiled, reaching over to tuck a strand of hair behind Ruby's ear. "I would most certainly say the same about you. Not just here, but anytime I'm with you."

"Oh, you're just saying that." Ruby bumped shoulders with her girlfriend, grinning from ear to ear.

"No, really. You make me feel so different than I used to. I feel free. I feel happy. I feel like..." Leanna paused, searching for the right words. "I feel like I'm experiencing love, *real* love. Except, every time feels like the first time all over again. Does that make sense?" Leanna asked with a shy chuckle.

Ruby nodded eagerly. "It does! And I'm so happy to hear it... I know I didn't know you for long before we got together, but you've only seemed to get happier the longer we've been together. Feels like maybe we're doing something right." She shrugged with that same beaming smile.

"Well, of course! You've done wonders with our business, after all," Leanna teased with a wink, leaning in to kiss Ruby on her burning cheek.

"Come on, Leanna," Ruby mumbled, still smiling through her blush. Despite her timidness, Ruby turned herself to better face Leanna, resting her hands on the nape of her neck and eying her gorgeous lips with a soft and gentle yearning.

Leanna leaned in, barely brushing her lips against Ruby's before whispering against them, "You've been happy too, right?"

"Happier than ever," Ruby hummed, tilting her head and pulling Leanna down for a deeper kiss.

Leanna happily followed, kissing Ruby slow and sweet as the light around them began to fade with the sun. She pulled at Ruby's lips once more before taking a slow and silent breath.

"One moment," Leanna whispered, pulling

back and letting her fingertips trail along Ruby's cheek as she stepped back.

Ruby's brow furrowed slightly, watching Leanna with a quiet confusion, but she kept her mouth closed and waited patiently as Leanna reached into one of her pockets.

"Ruby," Leanna whispered into the cool air.

The woman gave Leanna her full attention. Her curiosity, blushing cheeks, and dazzling green eyes were making Leanna fall in love all over again.

"I'd like to make you even happier than you are now," Leanna started, slowly lowering herself to one knee. "If you'll have me, despite my faults, I promise to always give you my best and to fall in love with you again every single day."

Ruby took a step back, eyes wide and hands delicately covering her open mouth.

"Will you marry me?" Leanna asked, opening a small box to reveal a diamond ring with a silver band, decorated with tiny silver snowflakes. Leanna let the grace and elegance fall away as she waited for the answer to the one thing that would mean so much more than the business she spent so long working for. Ruby was worth ten times all the work she'd put into The Fox Retreats, and then some.

Ruby's eyes were blinking fast, and she nodded quickly once, then twice, then pushed herself forward to wrap her arms around Leanna's neck and hold her tight, nearly sending her tumbling to the ground.

"Yes!" Ruby laughed through her tears, squeezing Leanna tight. "I'd love that! More than anything."

THANK YOU FOR READING MY BOOK!

It really means a lot to me and I hope you enjoyed delving into the story of Leanna and Ruby.

Join my mailing list and be first to hear about my next book, https://mailchi.mp/2a09276da35f/ graceparkeswrites I promise I don't spam :)

Want to get in touch? Feel free to email me directly on graceparkeswrites@hotmail.com
You can find me on social media
Instagram - @graceparkesauthor
TikTok - @graceparkesauthoe
X - @graceparkesfic

Printed in Great Britain
by Amazon